FINDING GRAND

Tim Holsten

ISBN: 0692738827
ISBN 13: 9780692738825
Library of Congress Control Number: **XXXXX (If applicable)**
LCCN Imprint Name: Outrigger Books

To the awe-inspiring community of friends that surrounds our family.

DAY 1

1. 1979

Leaning fully horizontal over the handrail, I felt like throwing up my El Tovar granola. I guesstimated it would travel at least a few hundred yards, bouncing off the sheer, cream-colored Kaibab limestone wall, before landing on a ledge and getting eaten by an unlucky chipmunk with a poor sniffer. It occurred to me that I would not be throwing up at, but *in*, the Grand Canyon. Was this National Park sacrilege? My backpack frame kept whacking the back of my head, exacerbating a headache and blurring a famous view, presently wasted on me, into the vast nothingness. I was self-conscious of being in plain view of all of the other early morning hikers entering the Bright Angel trail, most sucking down nicotine as if it were an energy source. Nearby I could hear the light-saber sound effects my best friend Chad always made while urinating. Anticipating the vigor needed for today's ten-mile trek to the bottom, I had conservatively paced myself in the El Tovar Lounge last night on Miller Lite. That was, until Chad had the cockamamie idea to kick off his bachelor party weekend with countless rounds of shots.

During a temporary pause in my nausea, I slowly raised my upper torso above the handrail to an upright position, while remaining mindful of a headache that amplified with movement. When the shoulder, chest, and waist straps of my backpack constricted in response to my body's fulcrum shift, the jolt made my head swell. As I turned away from the railing, I closed my eyes and tried to find a happy place back inside the haven of youth and college, even though both of those memberships expired last week.

My pack, top-heavy with water gallons and a case of Miller Lite, tugged my listless body two uncontrolled stutter steps backwards, connecting my butt with the handrail. My eyes opened wide in horror as gravity continued to pull the top of the pack, towing my body with it. With nothing to stunt my momentum, I began flipping backwards over the railing. Blinded by the rising sun in a clear June sky, I frantically fumbled with my buckles. When my pack was entirely suspended over the canyon, my left hiking boot rose off the ground. Fuck! This would be one of those idiotic, preventable deaths. I would never progress beyond son, student, or temporary boyfriend. I *really* wanted to see next year's sequel to *Star Wars*. Like a child in his initial shock from pain, I released a soundless scream as my second boot left the trail.

2. 2001

E xit north out of San Diego, scale the mountains between Temecula and Palm Springs, speed across desolate desert roads, hang a right at Lake Havasu, cross through the freight-train valleys of northern Arizona, and take a left in Williams. No pulling over for curiosities, like the Route 66 museums or Bedrock City, a replica of Fred Flintstone's hometown, because this trip was not about the journey, only the destination, a paradigm shift I feared paralleled our lives. Conversation was minimal and the awkward silence had long ago been accepted. I killed any unnecessary comments before letting them escape. We could trade thoughts and stories about our kids—were they still *kids* in college?—but this had served as filler so often that every morsel had been devoured. A seventies rock radio station filled the void.

I tried to identify the shortest of the three lines at the park entrance. As my window went down, cool air blew in. A *Close Encounters of the Third Kind* Richard Dreyfuss with sideburns lookalike ranger stuck his head out of the booth, collected my ten dollars, and gave us a pass and map.

"Are you sure you want to visit today?" he asked. "Visibility is zero zero."

"We'll be fine," I told the guy who landed the lead in *Encounters* after McQueen, Hoffman, Pacino, Hackman, and Nicholson turned it down.

It was interesting that a park employee tried to talk us out of entering a perfectly open park. I remembered how sad the *Rides Closed Today* posting at Disneyland made me feel as a child. And how it was strategically placed inside, not outside, of the turnstiles.

A dense fog had settled on the road and surrounding pines ever since we ascended out of Tusayan. I turned on my headlights to help split the pea soup. Visibility was limited, but could it truly be the ominous sounding *zero zero*, whatever that designation meant? We proceeded with caution, and my inner excitement built and senses heightened as we neared *it*. We passed the left turnoff to the park accommodations and amenities, and then the right to the Desert View area, and continued on towards the visitor center parking lot. It was sparsely populated—not a surprise on a cold, off-season December day. After delicately hauling our cramped legs out of the high-backed swiveling bucket seats of my maroon '75 Cutlass, a car I had owned since college, we each slipped on another layer and headed in the opposite direction of the visitor center.

The walkway was covered with a fine layer of moisture that would slicken if the temperature dropped any further. Our anticipation countered the extra weight of worry we had been carrying for some time. As we neared the Mather Point rocky outcrop and view area, an oncoming younger couple shared an unsolicited *maybe tomorrow* comment. Even before we ventured on to the jetty of rock named after the first director of the National Park Service, Stephen Mather, the disappointment set in. We stepped carefully on the slippery Kaibab limestone—missteps here gave you a heart attack. Stopping at the protective railings, attempting to attain eastern, northern, and western views, the results were consistent.

"Couldn't have predicted *this*, Fiver," Mae commented, using an ancient pet name for me.

The *Titanic* could have been docked a stone's throw in front of us and we would be oblivious. Could illusionist Doug Henning be playing a trick on us? Even leaning over the railing and staring straight down, something I would normally avoid due to the mysterious magnetic pull of the bottom, I could only see the first twenty-five yards of the slope immediately below. Mae exhibited an indifferent look, the default through her forties. Two hundred seventy-seven miles long, eighteen miles wide, nearly a mile deep, and the Grand Canyon was nowhere to be seen.

3. '79

As my human teeter-totter progressed, my hands gave up on unbuckling and shot out for invisible handholds. Images of my harrowing plummet and skeleton-shattering impact tortured my mind and paralyzed my reflexes. I could not have scripted a worse way to leave this world.

When my plank reached forty-five degrees, I felt a searing pain just below my neck as something clawed at my chest strap. My body jerked as the flipping momentum arrested, then reversed as something fiercely tugged me back towards equilibrium. My right boot touched earth, then my left, and then the weight of the pack slammed against my body, buckling my knees and crashing me forward to the trail. Someone's arm withdrew across my chest as my hands splayed out to break my fall. Gravel painfully left its impression in my palms and knees. Staring down, in a tripod position, I unbuckled my straps and violently heaved the pack off. A Miller Lite can dribbled out the top and rolled down the trail. Hikers paused to watch this unnatural occurrence in a natural setting, and it rewarded them by exploding ten yards later. An amplified sense of awareness and euphoria from surviving a near death experience overruled my previous headache.

I stood up slowly to confront my savior. Looking directly into the low sun, I was blinded by the light, but not *revved up like a deuce | another runner in the night* (or more commonly sung as, *wrapped up like a douche | when you're rollin' in the night*). When I was able to ascertain details by squinting, I recognized the outline of a female, backlit with glowing borders. I shielded my eyes with my left hand and observed her long, dark brown hair, pulled back by a mustard headband, framing her fair-skinned face, animated and smiling, high on saving a life. She had espresso eyes, a freckled nose, and soft, full lips and cheeks, which connected at impactful dimples. Her soft curves continued through a white embroidered peasant top, cutoff jeans, and well-worn hiking boots. She looked like Linda Blair, the recent young adult version I saw in a preview for the upcoming movie *Roller Boogie*, not the child whose head spun around in *The Exorcist*.

My most heartfelt *thank you* was ready on the launching pad when an elongated, thick brown head with stretched ears rudely interrupted my civilities. The mule, carrying a tourist, parked between the girl and me and stared at me curiously. After much *shooing*, it descended down the trail followed by a barren of five more, and as the last crossbred offspring of a male donkey and female horse passed, I sadly discovered that the Linda Blair doppelgänger had disappeared.

"Ready to go?" Chad asked from behind, in his gravelly, Wolfman Jack–like voice.

I turned around to see my friend struggling to pull up the zipper of his OP cord shorts. Chad's long, sandy blond Björn Borg haircut rivaled my shaggy brown Jimmy Connors style. For intimidation factor, Chad even wore Björn's trademark white headband with a red stripe flanked by two blue ones. We both complemented our tees and cord shorts with hiking boots and tube socks.

He hadn't witnessed the near fall, and when I recapped I could tell he assumed I was exaggerating. He offered me six-thirty in the morning beef jerky, which I turned down, and then helped me get my pack back on. He then turned around and asked me to push the play button on his black Sanyo radio and cassette player, which was bungee'd to his pack. The stockier Chad was shorter than I by a half foot at five foot six and, even though our hard-frame packs were already heavy with our weekend living and boozing necessities, he insisted on bringing his tunes.

The high-pitched opening guitar riff of Creedence Clearwater Revival's "Up Around the Bend" echoed throughout the canyon as we began our descent. Even though I still mourned the band's breakup, John Fogerty's gritty baritone kicked off our trek in style: *There's a place up ahead and I'm goin' | just as fast as my feet can fly.*

One of the mule guides hauled ass—his own—up the trail yelling at Chad to cut the music, before we even reached the soulfully delivered first chorus. It turned out loud music was against park rules and, in addition to potentially annoying other visitors, it spooked the mules, which on a trail full of precipices could be lethal. We turned if off, but then turned it back on at a lower volume as soon as the guide was out of earshot; Chad was not going to let his preconceived soundtrack moment be ruined.

Though the views into the big fissure in the Colorado Plateau were more inspiring, I gazed downward at the five-foot-wide dirt path carved out of the sheer hillside, overly paranoid of a misstep. The Bright Angel trail was originally built by Havasupai Indians as a water access route through a fault that bisected the canyon. It ended up being owned for many years by a white man who charged a one-dollar toll to tourists, before the National Park Service took over the land. It was now the canyon's superhighway.

Chad and I knew a lot of Grand Canyon trivia after taking a San Diego State University fluff class, *The History of National Parks*, in our final semester. We took it because our fraternity had all of the old exams in the house library: a file cabinet with tests, papers, well-worn *Playboy*s, and a *How To* book on growing weed. Both of us got surprisingly engrossed in the subject's majestic scenery, key figures like John Muir, and stories of adventure. Extra course emphasis was put on Yellowstone, Yosemite, and the fifteenth park—GC. The only disappointment was learning Jellystone—Yogi and Boo Boo's address—was fictional.

We made a pact during the semester to, shortly after graduation, drive the eight hours to the canyon, stay at the historic El Tovar, hike the ten miles into the basin, and hang out a few days at the remote, historic Phantom Ranch. With Chad's wedding slated for the end of June, he justified to his sorority sweetheart this would be a safe, innocent, and memorable bachelor party with his best friend. Then, outside of her earshot, he told me we would be perpetually drunk, hike on psychedelics, and hire a stripper for Phantom Ranch. After a discussion about basic human safety and the rarity of strippers who were willing to hike twenty round-trip miles, Chad agreed to simply get drunk and bring some good tunes. It was a textbook example of the checks and balances system I routinely employed to keep him out of trouble.

We stopped in front of a trail sign with safety warnings: Off-trail hiking could result in long falls without soft landings, and over-heating and under hydrating could result in potentially lethal heat exhaustion. It would be twenty degrees warmer a mile down in the basin, and even though the sun just woke up, the rim was already well into the sixties. The sign also cautioned hikers to stand on the inside of the trail when mules passed. My fuzzy morning brain was not able to process what was considered the *inside* of the trail.

Chad and his disproportionate tree stump legs, which powered our football team to an interfraternity championship, led the way and aimed to keep a healthy pace. We hoped to cover the eight-mile descent to the Colorado River in three hours, and the additional two miles to Phantom Ranch in one more. The upper portion of the trail contained long switchbacks bordered by steep drops and vast openness. My earlier near-fall kept me *on* edge away from *the* edge. My thoughts were focused inward, wondering if my brush with death would prove a catalyst for answers, or, at least, clues, to what had freshly been all-consuming—my unknown direction in life after graduating.

Towards the end of the long first cut, while I chugged water due to my new fear of heat exhaustion, the trail passed through a rock tunnel. Exiting the other side, I smiled for the first time in the young day—I rediscovered my rescuer, a couple hundred yards out, descending the next switchback. A wide-brimmed round straw hat now shaded her face, and she was hiking with an extremely large person wearing a cowboy hat. *Large* was an understatement. At first, from the muscular, wide-shouldered, six-and-a-half-foot-plus stature in a gray tank top, I assumed it was a dude, but after further focusing, which was difficult for my brain and eyes to cooperate on, I noticed the long strawberry blonde hair draped over her pack and tan, strong, yet shapely, telephone poles sprouting out of her cutoff jeans.

Chad had also taken notice of the two girls and was laughing at something. I caught up to him and he pointed towards the towering one, who was grooving her arms to Chad's tunes, which he had me turn up a few more decibels back at the warnings sign. Her arms were rolling, drumming, pointing, flapping, and clapping to Creedence's "Who'll Stop the Rain," which carried easily across the canyon's openness. I pointed at her hiking partner and told Chad she was the one who saved me at the railing.

Misjudging the direction of my point, Chad asked, "The beefy one?"

His Wolfman voice amplified and, to my horror, the *beefy one* glanced uphill at us. I stared intensely at the horizon to avoid eye contact. When I eventually lowered my eyes, her friend in the wide-brimmed hat met them. She was smiling. Knowing it would not take much volume, I weakly yelled *thank you* towards her, and although I could not see her lips move, *you're welcome* arrived as a warm whisper in my ear.

4. '01

In my younger years, when someone mentioned the word *hotel*, I thought only of the red plastic *Monopoly* piece, approximately twice as big as the green house. In my adult years, I thought only of this place, the El Tovar. While Mae and I had stayed in many establishments, this one, located a mere twenty feet from the south rim, was our first together—and possibly our last.

At the front desk, I asked the young blonde with Farrah Fawcett–feathered hair whether it was common for the canyon to be wholly concealed like it was today. She said *sometimes*, followed by awkward silence, and I opined this was not her area of expertise. As she retrieved the key, I glanced nervously at the javelina, mounted on the large dark-stained pine beams, staring my way with tusks ready to pierce. Taxidermy was a consistent theme throughout the rustic hunting lodge–vibed busy lobby, as were paintings of the canyon, southwestern Indian accents, and craft furniture. Born in 1905, the El Tovar was only four years away from celebrating its centennial birthday.

Mae finished up a phone call and told me the Barretts' escrow closed. Before I even asked, she confirmed Lucinda, our assistant, had delivered their closing gift. Through the open-air center rotunda, I watched the bellhop carry our bags up the stairs to our third floor canyon-view room. We followed, after walking by the cocktail lounge responsible for a long-ago hangover, which had been integral to our original, chance meeting.

I noticed they switched out the rotary phones with the more efficient push button models in our basic, no frills room with blue carpet, stately older-looking furniture, and canyon-themed art. The positioning of the hotel was intended to offer most rooms an angled glimpse into the canyon. Today, I could see only the grounds leading up to the rim, and then the nothingness. I suggested to Mae we get a caffeine boost at the Bright Angel Coffee Shop, but she preferred a nap. I assumed she wanted some personal space even though she asked me to join her.

I walked the rim trail past the Kachina and Thunderbird lodges to the Bright Angel Lodge. My lungs and wounded ego could feel the effects of the cool weather and nearly 7,000-foot elevation. Like the El Tovar, the Bright Angel interior was bustling with activity as a result of the lack of external scenery. After eight hours in the car I had no desire to stay inside. I took my large light-roast coffee and continued west on the rim trail past The Lookout, a rubble stone observatory/gift shop on the canyon edge, and then past Kolb Studio, once home to pioneer photographers Ellsworth and Emery Kolb, who took shots of tourists riding mules down into the canyon. I walked to the head of the Bright Angel trail, usually the most popular spot in the park.

The fog gave the illusion it would erase anyone who entered the lengthy trail down to the Colorado River. The unknown made me feel so incredibly vulnerable. When I was younger I had an easier time taking on the unknown and understanding what I could, or could not, change. With age, I lost the ability and confidence to tell the difference, and more often than not followed the path of least resistance. Due to this constant avoidance, it often felt like the unknown in my life had grown like an untreated cancer, and if I never regained the courage to attempt to change, it could have dire consequences. I tentatively leaned over the waist-high handrail and stared down into the hidden abyss. A pivotal, fortuitous, yet haunting, memory forced me to quickly back away.

The declining light of early evening made the fog more ominous as I walked the rim trail back to the El Tovar. An employee was hanging Christmas lights over the hotel entrance. I was surprised to find Mae on a couch by the crackling fireplace in the lobby reading her book, *The World According to Garp*, under the watchful eyes of two bull elks. This confirmed, at least in my mind, she had simply craved independent time.

"Any good?" I asked as I approached.

"Interesting, but I don't know if I'd call it good," she said. "There's a scene you'd hate."

"I heard about it. I'm not reading it." I had overprotective tendencies, which prevented me from reading or watching anything where harm came to a child.

"Dinner?" I asked with artificial enthusiasm. We both suffered from a loss of appetite due to the oppressive stress.

"Sure."

The dining room, which could seat a couple hundred, was near full, no doubt because there was nothing touristy competing with it. It was a simple, huge open room flanked, like a sports field by its goals, by two blazing stone fireplaces. The choice view seats were on the north end by the large picture windows, but on a foggy night they were all the same. We were seated in the middle.

"Where are you folks from?" the waiter asked.

"San Diego," Mae said.

"Sorry about the weather today," he said.

"It's okay. We came here to relax anyway," Mae said.

Liar. We came here to try to save our marriage. We came here to try to find kindling for a dying flame. We came here to see if our fire was even worth burning. We came here, not other favorites like Santa Barbara, Carmel, or San Francisco, because this place inspired us. Great things happened here. *We* happened here.

From a menu that had evolved little, if any, from the first time I ate here, she ordered trout and I got the New York strip. When she requested only water and no adult beverage, I knew she wanted to stay on task with organic conversation, so I followed suit. There were no canyon highlights to discuss since we could not even prove it was there. The lack of visibility itself could provide fodder, but how many different ways could you describe *nothing*? I could point out interesting Indian art pieces, but that seemed too trivial.

We picked at our food, for sustenance, not satisfaction. I could see the yearning in her eyes. She wanted what we used to have. She wanted it to flow, yet be unpredictable. She wanted the birth of new ideas that could grow into future experiences. She wanted an interesting perspective on topical situations. She wanted a faith-based opinion. When did I stop giving her these things, and why? Were her expectations too high, and mine too low? Why was our whole life together a blur?

By six-thirty, our conversation dipped to discussing our favorite movies from the year we met—hers was *Norma Rae*, I said mine was *The Warriors*, though it was really *The Champ*. It was a dead-end topic, and the uncomfortable silence after had us flagging our arms for the check. I suggested we grab drinks in the lounge. She suggested we instead go back up to the room to relax. It was the safest and least adventurous thing we could do, very uncharacteristic for the Mae I first met. At what point in our relationship did she become so submissive? Was it my fault, or by choice? There was nothing good on TV at seven. What night was it? Friday, I think. Yes, Friday for sure. Friday nights made me think of *Wonder Woman*. *Wonder Woman* made me think of...yes, I was ready to go upstairs.

5. '79

Even in early summer, on trail sections never exposed to the sun, we encountered muddy patches and desolate ice flanked by greenery—life was determined by exposure. Motivation from my recent exposure to death was steadily conquering my hangover, bootprint by bootprint, and we had closed most of the gap to the two girls. I should have been more focused on *why* I was saved instead of by whom.

We passed through another rock tunnel and began a series of tighter switchbacks. As Creedence crooned "Long As I Can See the Light" and the giant girl continued to hand jive, the Zorro-carved path allowed for a lot of glance stealing, at least on my part. A large sheer wall of white Coconino sandstone formed on our right. The Grand Canyon was comprised of layers, visual stripes, of disparate rock, deposited from ancient oceans and buried one on top of another. These hidden layers were pushed skyward as part of the Colorado Plateau landmass, then revealed when the Colorado River patiently eroded and carved its way through them. Our hike, which began in the canyon's bathtub ring of cream-colored Kaibab limestone, would drop us through more than a dozen different layers. Throughout the day, while we avoided missteps in mule deposits, we would notice the trail's dirt color shifting with each layer.

We neared a resthouse at the mile-and-a-half mark, an open-air structure with four stacked-rock pillars supporting a gabled wood roof with exposed beams. It would offer a shaded rest and was one of the few trail stops at which to refill water. A handful of others took pause inside, including the two girls, who were sitting on a bench with their packs off.

"Are you in the Delta house?" the large arm-flapper asked Chad loudly—comic book bubble three exclamation mark loudly—as we approached. She was mocking his purple shirt with green Greek lettering.

"No, Lambda Chi Alpha. San Diego State Chapter," Chad, unfazed, said proudly. He appreciated aggressive behavior.

"Right on," she practically shouted, continuing her comic book persona, making me wonder about her true identity. The center of her tank was branded with a bold red, white, and blue letter *A*.

"And, are you?" the other one asked me. A soothing lilt in her voice disarmed me.

"Yes. I'm in the same house," I said.

"No. Are you?" She looked at my shirt and smiled. Her dimpled cheeks broke through another of my layers.

I glanced down at my white *I'm a Pepper* t-shirt. "They were giving these away at a campus taste test."

"So, what are you going to do with your second chance at life?" the bigger one asked me. She was much cuter than I initially sized her up to be. She looked liked *The Waltons'* middle daughter, Erin, although her brother was more likely basketball player Bill rather than John-Boy.

"What do you mean?" I asked.

"Since Mae saved you."

I smiled at her friend, Mae. "I hadn't figured out what to do with my first chance," I said.

"Sorry about that," Mae said, and pointed at my shirt collar.

I touched my skin there and it was tender. I pulled my collar out and looked down to see a cat-like scratch across my upper chest.

"This will be a good reminder," I said. "I'm Kevin, and this is my friend and," I said mockingly, "my *frat bro*, Chad."

"I'm Anne. And, of course, you and Mae already physically met," the larger one said. "Did you guys see the petroglyphs along the rock just past the first tunnel?"

"I was too distracted by your grooving," Chad said. "You're a freak of nature. What do you use all that muscle for?"

"I'm a shotputter at U of A," Anne said, also unfazed. Apparently, she too appreciated aggressive behavior. "Man, how many packs a day do you smoke to get your voice like that?"

"None, foxy, this is my natural voice," Chad said. "So how far can you toss it?"

"Over seventy feet. Should make the Olympic team next year. Moscow, here I come."

I stumbled slightly when I took my pack off and sat down.

"Are you okay?" Mae asked me.

"Just a little hungover."

"Better keep hydrated," she said. Her nurse-like concern triggered instinctual patient feelings.

"You got drunk in a National Park? Who does that?" Anne asked.

"We do, Mama," Chad said. "We closed down the El Tovar Lounge last night. Tapped out their Miller Lite keg. You gals stay there?"

"No, we got here this morning," Anne said. "We're heading down to the Bright Angel campgrounds at the bottom for the weekend. How about you?"

"We're spending the weekend right next to you in the Phantom Ranch cabins," Chad said.

I noticed Anne slyly poke a finger into Mae's side. Mae acknowledged it, but did not comment.

"You both go to U of A?" I asked.

"Just finished our junior year," Mae said. "What year are you guys?"

It felt like a typical early evening college bar conversation—unadventurous questions before drinks kicked in. Only, it was eight in the morning, and instead of a neon Miller sign as a backdrop, Anne and Mae were framed by a view so majestic, it seemed fake.

"We graduated last week," I said.

"Congratulations! Time to change the world. How are you going to do it?" Mae asked.

"I'm going to be a stockbroker and make a truckload of bread," Chad said.

"How altruistic," Mae said. "How about you?"

"I don't know yet," I said. "But I want to choose my career, instead of having it choose me, if that makes any sense. Maybe something meaningful where I can help people."

Her face became animated. I had captured her interest.

"Until I figure out what," I continued, "I'm going to work for my uncle selling real estate. I've worked there part-time all through college."

"Sounds great," she said, like an Eeyore balloon deflating.

I was not surprised by Mae's disappointment in my career indecision. I had hoped I would have more clarity on the topic by now. At our graduation ceremony in the Aztec Bowl stadium a few weeks ago, while Chad slept off a night in Tijuana in the seat next to me, I was moved by a Thomas Jefferson quote used in the commencement speech, "Nothing can stop the man with the right mental attitude from achieving his goal; nothing on Earth can help the man with the wrong mental attitude." It was a wake up call that I had too often been relying on the *wasn't-meant-to-be* crutch, instead of admitting I had more control over my environment. God didn't give me free will by mistake. Right then and there, while Chad awoke and relieved himself in an empty glass Gatorade bottle under his gown, I committed to retiring my youth's reserved attitude and adopting a more aggressive, goal-oriented one.

Though I felt impassioned about living a selfless life, I had no idea *whom* I would help or *how.* I assumed my schooling and family upbringing would have imprinted on me some sort of life roadmap, but the schooling was now in the rearview mirror, and I didn't feel my parents were equipped to give the directions I needed. All of my older male relatives had served in the military, and many of my friends' older brothers had fought, and died, in Vietnam. Even though there was no current draft, it was always in the back of my mind that at some point in my young life history would repeat itself and either some superpower would go on the offensive—maybe the Soviet Union—or we would stick our nose too far into where it didn't belong—Iran?

I pointed to an aptly named red rock ridgeline in the distance. "That butte is called Battleship Rock." While they were looking, I asked, "Has anyone tried the new electronic version of the board game?" No one had.

A large object shot horizontally through the sky across our line of vision. It was likely a bird of prey that had located its breakfast.

"What was that?" Chad asked.

"I think it was a Bermuda Ern," I said. Three brows furrowed and my obscure *Breakfast of Champions* book reference fell flat. Mae appeared to lose any potential interest in me, if she ever had any.

"Far out stereo, Wolfman," Anne said to Chad, without feeling the need to dignify my remark. "Cassettes are the future. Eight-tracks are dying like the dinosaurs."

"Thanks," he said. "Someone bought me one of those new Walkmans for graduation, but I exchanged it for this and a bunch of tunes. Can you believe those things cost two hundred bucks and you can only listen to your tunes with headphones? How antisocial. Nice fucking market research."

"What's up next?" Anne asked. "Stones, Who, Doors?"

"I didn't bring any of them," Chad said. He silently contemplated whether they were more worthy than the selections he brought.

"Got any disco?" Anne asked.

"Disco is pure crap. It won't last."

"Aren't you being a hypocrite?" Anne said.

"What are you talking about?"

"Look in a mirror. I assume your Björn Borg impersonation isn't accidental. He and Björn Ulvaeus of ABBA are probably best buds."

There was a look of terror in Chad's eyes as he realized for the first time Björn Borg and ABBA's members were all Swedish.

"What *did* you bring?" Anne asked.

"There's a San Francisco band I dig. Have you heard of Journey?"

"Right on. They're way decent. Pop them in, Björn."

Chad popped in Journey's *Infinity* tape, and Anne and Mae mounted their packs. As "Lights," the first track, kicked in and the girls departed, Anne raised her arms above her head and slowly waved them back and forth while singing along, *when the lights go down in the city*. Mae coupled a polite wave goodbye with an indifferent, unanimated glance.

I ate some beef jerky, which my stomach now craved instead of rejected, and Chad and I departed the resthouse, serenaded by the second track off *Infinity*, "Feeling That Way." It was a powerful song with dueling vocals from Gregg Rolie and the band's newest member, Steve Perry, who had a mind-blowing vocal range. Down the trail a bit we stopped to look at rust-colored pictographs on a cream-colored wall. A brother in our fraternity this year had an electronic game–playing machine, called a video computer system, and a prototype cartridge of the popular arcade game *Space Invaders*. His dad worked for Atari, the California company that made them. Many classes were missed while those absent destroyed these aliens, which looked eerily similar to some of these pictographs.

As we continued to follow comfortably behind the girls on an especially long, antisocial straightaway, Journey rudely received competition up trail from an escalating marching sound. I stopped and turned to identify the source. Chad, about ten yards behind me, did the same. Tramping towards us in a cloud of dust was a train of mules and their riders. They would overtake us shortly, so we parked to ease the process. Chad stood at the precipice side of the trail as they approached, also on the precipice side. The guide on the first mule signaled with his left hand for Chad to move to the other side of the trail. Now I knew what the *inside* of a trail was, so I moved. Chad, being Chad, signaled with his right hand that the mules should move to the other side—a battle of the asses had begun.

"Please move, sir," the guide, who looked like Latka from *Taxi*, shouted when he was within earshot.

I would have given the right of way to a creature three to four times my size. Chad would not let logic interfere with his stubbornness. It was not a sheer drop-off on the downhill edge where he stood so he was not risking his life, yet it was a steep slope you would prefer to avoid. The guide let his vehicle continue on its path of choice. Chad was forced off the trail and had to hold tight to a shrub to avoid tumbling away. It was an unfair standoff and, to add insult to injury, an older female rider commented, *we'll head 'em off at the pass, Borg.*

The girls had extended their lead on us and were out of sight. Chad, the betrothed, was not as concerned as I, the opportunist. While eating odd-looking trail mix, Chad complained the remaining way to the next resthouse, at the three-mile mark, about having more trail rights than *lazy, out of shape people who took pony rides.* When we neared the structure, which was almost identical to the last one, I was pleased to see Anne's profile obstructing an inordinate amount of the view through the open side.

23

"Don't get your hopes up. It's a big place," Mae said to Anne as we walked in.

"About us?" Chad interrupted.

"No, Kurt Russell. A ranger saw him yesterday," Mae said.

"The guy's a fucking Disney movie star. Who cares?" Chad said.

"Anne's been obsessed since he played Elvis in the TV movie," Mae said.

"I'm not obsessed," said Anne. "I wouldn't kick him out of bed, though."

"I imagine he'd leave on his own accord as soon as he sobered up," Chad said.

"Kiss my grits," Anne said, laughing.

"No can do," Chad said. "I'm off the market. Getting married this month. Kevin's horny, though."

I reddened and put my hand over Chad's mouth. The girls congratulated him as we took our packs off and sat.

"No sorority house sweetheart?" Mae asked me mockingly.

"Nothing that's ever gotten too serious."

"He keeps getting dumped," Chad added.

"Why?" Mae asked.

"They weren't meant to be, I guess," I said.

"That is the lamest phrase, *meant to be*," Mae said.

"Why?" I asked.

"Because relationships are hard and need to be worked on. They're not a coincidental meeting you should bail on the moment things get tough. Right?" Mae aimed her question at Chad, who was busy smelling his pits.

"Mine's easy," Chad said. "Almost too easy at times."

"Do you worry about missing out on something else—better or different—by getting married so young?" Mae asked.

"Of course I do. Every day," he said. "But I worry more about what my fiancée, Suzy, and I would be *missing out* on *together*."

"What's your status?" I asked Mae.

"Single and independent by choice," she said. It was the same insecure answer I often gave.

"What's your story?" Chad asked Anne. "When you're not having your way with Kurt, of course."

"I seem to be eternally single," she said with a sad smile. "I'm hopeful, but realistic."

"You're too hard on yourself," Mae said.

"I'll say," Chad said. "You're a monument all by yourself."

"Thanks," Anne said hesitantly to the ambiguous remark.

"Show of hands," Mae said, "parents still together?"

Chad and Anne's hands went up.

"Congratulations," Mae said to both of them. "You've been conditioned to avoid divorce."

"Why would you say that?" I asked. "I'm going to avoid the mistakes my parents made."

"And what were those mistakes?" she asked.

I could not think of anything specific. "They didn't have enough in common anymore. They grew apart."

"So they were never in love?" she asked.

"Of course they were. They got married."

"And that wasn't enough of a foundation to build off of?"

"I guess not," I said weakly.

"Yeah. Sounds like you've got it figured out."

"What about your parents?" I asked.

"They didn't give it enough effort. They also didn't handle adversity well."

"Like what?" I asked. I noticed Anne dropped her head.

Mae paused before answering. "I guess some kids are tougher than others to raise."

I did not know whether she was talking about herself or a sibling, but could tell this was going deeper than our few minutes together merited.

"Have you always had a good relationship with your parents?" she asked me.

"A *great* relationship, with both of them."

"So they've worked hard at being *great* parents?"

"Absolutely."

"You're an only child, aren't you? I'll bet their world revolves around you."

"I am. But no, it doesn't," I said defensively.

"So...how did they end up in a better relationship with you than with each other? I think we learn more from our parents' behavior than from what they try to teach us. *And the cat's in the cradle and the silver spoon....*"

I blanked and averted her stare. My eyes focused outside the resthouse on the remains of an old cable car system that used to bring supplies down to our next stop, Indian Garden. I realized I had spent my whole life grading my parents on the wrong scale. If I had some type of futuristic long-range walkie-talkie device, I'd call them right now and ask Mae's question. Divorce was so commonplace amongst my friends' parents that I perceived it to be as natural of an ending as success. When my eyes returned to Mae, her grin changed in the weirdest of ways.

"Your tooth moved," I said.

"What did you say?" Chad asked.

"Mae's tooth just moved," I said.

We all looked to Mae, who smiled widely, showing her complete set of whites. One of her upper teeth, next to her front two, dropped a centimeter, leaving a black hole above it. A second later it ascended back.

"How in the fuck did you do that?" Chad asked.

"I have a retainer with a fake tooth attached to it," she said. "In a few months I'm getting a permanent implant."

"How'd you lose the real one?" I asked.

"Oh, oh, oh, let me tell it," Anne said excitedly.

"Go ahead," Mae said. "You always find it more entertaining than I do."

26

"So, we were at a frat party a few months ago," Anne said. "Mae was infatuated with this Kappa Sig named Thor, seriously, Thor, who looked like a beefed up version of the guy who played the older *Hardy Boy*. They were serving plastic cups of Miller Lite with live goldfish in them. Not wanting to disappoint Thor, Mae, an environmentalist, drained it." Anne laughed heartily, and her giddiness prevented the story's conclusion.

Chad and I looked at each other, puzzled, not able to connect the dots.

"And?" I asked.

"And being an environmentalist and needlessly killing a live fish," Mae finished monotonously, probably for the *n*th time, "I felt like I had been possessed by the devil. I tried to exorcise it as fast as possible."

"You made yourself puke?" Chad asked.

"Correct. I ran to the bathroom, crouched over the toilet, jammed my fingers down my throat, and released the fish back to the sea. During the process, my head lurched into the porcelain rim and I chipped my two front teeth and knocked this lateral incisor out."

"Did your head…" Chad began.

"No," Mae interrupted. "My head did not spin around like Linda Blair's."

We were all smiling.

"It's a little late," I said, "but I highly doubt a goldfish has the survival skills to navigate the sewer back to the sea from Arizona."

"I thought of that after the fact," she said.

"Also, it was a frat house toilet," I said. "You probably didn't need to jam your fingers down your throat to throw up. Could have just taken in the view."

"Thanks for the advice," Mae said with a disgusted look. "Anyway, I have a bad habit of constantly playing with the retainer with my tongue."

Lucky retainer.

"Awesome story!" Chad said. His smirk matched the perma-grin he wore for a week after we saw *Animal House*.

Seeing how impressed we were with the comically tragic tale, Anne added, "I once jumped so high at a party that I busted my head open on a mirrored disco ball. Nineteen stitches." She pulled her hair back to reveal a three-inch hairline scar on the side of her forehead.

"That's what you get for listening to that crap," Chad said.

The disappointment on Anne's face indicated this was not her desired response. I recognized a fragile eagerness to please.

"Hike safely, boys," Mae said, stood, and took a hearty swig from her canteen.

Anne poured water over her head and then mounted her pack without drinking anything. I saw Chad's eye dart to the drenched upper portion of her tank top.

"Better drink some," Chad told her, looking nowhere near her eyes. "It's gonna be a scorcher."

"I drank plenty earlier. I'm like a camel," she said, regaining her volume and swagger, not bothered by his wayward stare.

"Kevin, didn't I say it smelled like camel back there?" Chad asked. I ignored him.

"Thanks for the Chautauqua," I said to Mae and Anne as they hiked out. It was another unrecognized obscure reference, this time from the book *Zen and the Art of Motorcycle Maintenance*, which fell on deaf ears. Although as she left, Mae's eyes conveyed curiosity.

Chad and I exited the three-mile resthouse five minutes later to "Ballroom Blitz," the first track off Sweet's *Desolation Boulevard* album. We soon came upon Jacob's Ladder, a steep mile of tight switchbacks, often with carved-out stairs, through the Redwall and Muav limestone layers. The girls were already a few rungs down, although Anne's whirling arms proved they were well within earshot.

"And she's buying a stairway to heaven," Chad said as he peered down the incline. He lost his balance, then retreated to the inside of the trail. The butte resembling a battleship loomed large above us on our left. Chad led, but his gait was uncharacteristically slow and tentative—Chad did not do *anything* tentative. He was also hiking so far on the inside of the trail that his uphill boot kept stepping on uneven ground. I was about to heckle him, but then he stopped walking, turned in a full circle with his mouth hanging open, took his pack off, and sat his butt down in the red dirt.

"What are you doing?" I asked and stopped.

He looked up at me in a weird way, as if I were hard to find.

"Give me a minute," he said. He ejected the *Desolation Boulevard* tape, put it in his pack, then rummaged around and pulled out a generic-looking tape with *Tender Chad* written on it.

"What's that?" I asked.

"A mixed tape Suzy made me," he said.

"What's a *mixed tape?*"

"She copied songs from different artists onto the same tape."

"Far out."

He popped it in and "All By Myself," a ballad by Eric Carmen, began.

"Are you kidding?" I asked.

"Just wait," he said, and froze, staring into the nothingness with bug-like eyes.

I glanced down the slope and noticed the girls had stopped and were looking up at us, equally confused by the drastic change in tempo.

When the song got to the first chorus, Eric Carmen *and* Chad bawled, *all by myself | don't want to be | all by myself | anymore.* The duet carried crisply down the Bright Angel Fault.

He was about to repeat the chorus when I waved my hand in front of his face, scaring him into falling over on his side.

"What's wrong with you?" I asked as he slowly sat up and marveled at the red dirt on his palms.

"Oh, shit!" I said. "What are you on?"

6. '01

The moment we crossed the threshold of our room, I blurted it out, *do you wanna have sex*—no spontaneous move or romantic gesture, just the get-to-the-point question. I was convinced that if I never asked for it, I would no longer do this activity, at least not alone.

"I knew you were thinking that. Sure. Let me brush my teeth first."

I sat on the bed and waited for her to finish what she recently considered foreplay. I knew she would prefer I brush mine also, but it felt weird interrupting primal urges with calculated little circles. When she was done brushing, flossing, washing her face, attempting to extract the contents of a blackhead, and going to the bathroom, all with an indifferent look on her face, she apathetically moved on to the next task on her list, me, and the expression followed. She wanted to at least keep her top on, like our first time, but I pouted and she gave in.

Fully naked under the Indian blanket comforter, it did not take much contact to inspire me. Mae's natural beauty was as alluring as the day we met, though recent diminishing of facial and body curves, and shallowing of dimples, more stress than age driven, were noticeable. Even without the fog, this was the most awe-inspiring view in the National Park. Due to the infrequency I knew I would not last long, so I attempted to prolong the groping. Politely, but firmly, she insisted we move on to the next phase. I intently watched for her inner glow to illuminate our Indian blanket cocoon, but her dimmer switch had shorted out years ago. For one miniscule moment during our union, I felt she actually saw me, saw *us*, but I could not be sure. A minute later she was back in the bathroom. Why could it never be like our first time, which I measured every recurrence against? Recently, an unshakable, damaging image kept pushing to the forefront of my thoughts. In it Mae was experiencing her *next* first time. We had never been unfaithful to each other, and as far as I knew, neither of us had any desire to be, but this would be a repercussion if our marriage failed. It wasn't the physical act in the image that bothered me most—although it bothered me plenty—it was her smile, enjoyment, and glow, validating the emotion ran deeper.

When she returned to the bed with her *Garp* book, I was not sure what to do with myself because I did not bring anything to read. To watch hours of TV in a hotel room would be depressing.

"Would you like to talk about our stuff?" I asked.

"Honestly, honey, I'm too tired to process anything tonight. Can we talk about it tomorrow?"

"Of course," I said. The truth was, I did not want to talk about *it* at all. I wanted to snap my fingers and make *it* better. I wanted to wake up tomorrow in a new *it*, or original *it*, and forget about the real *it*.

"What are our TV options?" I asked. "*Donny and Marie? Diff'rent Strokes? Incredible Hulk? Dukes of Hazzard? Dallas?*"

"Did you just get asked by Richard Dawson on *Family Feud* to name the top Friday night TV shows from the late seventies?" Mae said, and smiled. This was a long-running gag of ours.

"Are you sure you don't want to go grab a drink?" I asked.

"I'd rather read."

"Do you mind if I head down for one?"

"If that's what you'd rather do, I'm fine with it."

The silent question mark in the middle of her statement generated guilt. Not enough, though.

"I'll be quick," I said.

7. '79

"Mushrooms," Chad said. "A couple stems and heads were in my trail mix."

I'd seen Chad like this before. I calculated I had been hired, at no cost, for about five hours of babysitting.

"Can you make it down?" I asked.

"I think so. I just need to get in a more relaxed state."

"By playing this crap tune?"

"It'll help me unwind. Suzy and I play this tape during sex."

I helped him stand up and get his pack back on. Due to the circumstances, I yielded to the tape choice, which continued to seduce the canyon. When I resumed hiking, I heard no accompanying footsteps. Chad had not moved and was peering down the slope, which was not sheer but offered a deadly tumble.

"Chad?"

He looked up and channeled Melissa Sue Anderson, who channeled the blind Mary Ingalls, as he tried to place me.

"I need your help," he said.

"Okay," I said, and walked back to him. "I'll walk next to you on the outside of the trail."

Chad reached an arm out in the direction of the vastness and quickly retracted it.

"Kevin," he said, "I want to hold your hand."

I laughed. "Buddy, I'll take care of you, but you don't need my hand."

"I seriously *need* to hold your hand," he said. His anxious expression and tone conveyed this request was no different than *I need food, I need water, I need oxygen,* or *I need to masturbate*—it was an essential.

I contemplated what an intelligent person would do in this situation. It felt like virginal territory and I would become the world's expert the minute I made a decision. Whether it was out of concern for my friend's safety, or the undeniable instinctual desire to pursue Mae, I could not say, but some force moved my right hand into his left, and he squeezed them together tightly. I looked down slope to the bottom of Jacob's Ladder to see if the girls had noticed and was relieved to see their heads facing forward. I gave Chad's hand a little tug and off we went.

I tried to mentally escape the situation, but Chad's continued singing made it difficult. "All By Myself" was followed by "Feelings," and when Morris Albert and Chad sang, *w-o-o-o feelings | w-o-o-o feelings,* his face shifted from frightened to goofy as his mind traveled to a happier place. Based on his lyrical accuracy, it was obvious Chad and Suzy's sex life was vigorous. I asked him if the sing-a-long was a necessity and, like the handholding—lucky me—it was.

It was during one of the "Feelings" choruses that the girls, who had finished the switchbacks and were now hiking through the relatively flat, widening valley of the Tonto Platform, stopped and, to my horror, pointed up at us on the highly exposed Ladder. Though their conversation was too far away to logically overhear, *fruits* somehow carried cleanly into my ear. I experimented letting go of Chad's hand and he wailed like Chewbacca in the trash compactor. With our pace reduced to a walk in the Park, and a reunion with the girls unlikely until we reached the campground and cabins, I would suffer hours of mental anguish until I could offer an explanation. Through the remaining rungs of the Ladder my daymare and Chad's cabaret continued, with Billy Joel and Chad declaring they love me *just the way you are*, and James Taylor and Chad gushing *how sweet it is to be loved by* me.

The environment changed drastically when the trail flattened out onto the pale green Bright Angel shale of the Tonto Platform, transitioning from the pinyon pines and Utah junipers of the upper cliffs to cactus and lower desert plants. Hiking across desert, and not cliff carving, I naturally assumed I could have my right hand back. Chewbacca's shriek, which interrupted Peaches and Herb and Chad singing about how good it felt to be *reunited*, suggested otherwise.

In the distance I could see our halfway point, the riparian green oasis of Indian Garden, where I hoped the girls would take an extended rest so I could explain this. I picked up the pace, with no objection from Chad's left hand, and kept both of us fueled up on water and jerky. We had only crossed paths with a few hikers so far and, prejudicially and thankfully, no one engaged us in conversation. The wide-open trail relaxed me. I contemplated how I could tell a politically correct version of this story as part of my best man's speech at his wedding. I was a little *too* relaxed. When Barbra Streisand and Chad complained *you don't bring me flowers | you don't sing me love songs*, Neil Diamond *and* I responded, *you hardly talk to me anymore | when you come through the door | at the end of the day*. I submissively let Barbra, Neil, and Chad handle the rest.

Familiar marching footsteps approached from behind as another mule train neared. Who knew what Chad saw coming, but the animals triggered a panic attack in him. He pulled me five—only five—yards off the trail, and had me crouch with him behind a two—only two—foot tall agave cactus. While Peter Frampton and Chad sang, because it did not occur to Chad, in hiding, to turn down the tunes or stop singing, *oh baby I love your way | everyday*, I hid in plain view of the passing mules and tourists with an angry scowl on my face. Chad was invisible.

We were well into side two of *Tender Chad* as we approached the crowded Indian Garden campgrounds, and I prayed that after Dionne Warwick and Chad finished proclaiming they knew they'll *never love this way again*, the tape would end. I heard, then saw, the first helicopter tour of the day high in the sky—could they discern the dual Adam's apples from that altitude? Indian Garden was a tangible mirage with a small spring feeding mature cottonwood trees and other greenery. It had been creatively named when someone realized Indians once gardened here. A light breeze rustled the green leaves, giving the trees a three-dimensional effect contrasted against the immovable backdrop of sand- and rust-colored mountains. The breeze carried the rich smell of campers' bacon through the high-seventies mid-morning air. For hikers turning around, or passing through, in addition to campsites there were a ranger station, mule corral, bathrooms, picnic benches, and all-important shade and water sources. Steps from the entrance, I casually attempted another hand separation, but Chewbacca squawked and squeezed it tighter. When the tape went silent for a few seconds, I smiled, thinking I averted a disaster. I felt I could at least endure the public handholding if Chad gave up his singing career. The music returned and my smile hastily retreated.

Three minutes later, after Olivia Newton-John and Chad had repeatedly confessed they were *hopelessly devoted* to me, the horrific experience was over. As long as I lived, I would never admit his rough voice blended nicely with her sweet one. Tourists had lined the parade route to watch, and listen to, our circus act of stupidity. The onlookers inhaled equal amounts of water, food, and smoke, in between their laughing fits. Multiple rangers deemed the event worthy enough to share on their walkie-talkies. Mae and Anne had been noticeably absent.

Of course, the exact moment we exited the throngs, a *click* signaled the end of side two and the public concert. Chad unceremoniously dropped my hand and asked me to put Sweet's *Desolation Boulevard* tape back in. With "Fox on the Run" blaring, our palm calluses no longer sandwiched, and Chad making nonsensical conversation, we began our final three miles to the river, gently sloping off the Tonto Platform along Garden Creek. When we reached Devil's Corkscrew, another series of steep switchbacks, this time through the dark red and black Vishnu schist layer of Pipe Canyon, my reprieve proved temporary as Chad's hand sought mine again, and *Tender Chad* gave an encore.

The growing static roar of the nearing river drew us through the last descent along Pipe Creek. When we reached the blue-green Colorado, the patient carver of the many layers of stubborn rock, the positive energy from the setting flowed through me and carved through my many layers of uncertainty. It made the problem of not knowing what I wanted to do with my life an inconsequential one. There was no place in the world I would rather be right now, albeit preferably without my fingers intertwined with Chad's, and without him and Lionel Richie telling me I was *once | twice | three times a lady.*

The Bright Angel trail changed names to the River trail, and we headed upstream towards the Silver Suspension Bridge, our three-hundred-foot crossing over to Phantom Ranch. My legs immediately felt the shift from gravity assisting them downhill on the hard path to the resistance of the rolling terrain containing patches of deep sand. It was approaching ninety degrees, and I saw pockets of distorted thick, warm air. I appreciated how the unfiltered sun lit up the colors of the canyon, but aside from the cottonwoods of Indian Creek, there were not a lot of places to hide from it. Chad abandoned his lounge act again due to the competing river thunder, and he even let me turn off the stereo. I continued to hold his hand, more to keep us on target than out of fear of Chewbacca's rage.

In the far distance a sand-colored pointed spire, the Zoroaster Temple butte, loomed over the canyon. With the Silver Suspension Bridge coming into focus, I heard a person's distress call, eclipsing the roar of the river. Running downstream on the trail towards us, in a cloud of dust, alone, wide-brimmed hat flopping, pack-less, excited, panicked, still radiant, Mae was yelling *help*.

8. '01

Looking back at me from the mirror-backed bar of the El Tovar Lounge was my dad's late seventies businessman haircut, identical to that of a male Lego head, that I swore I would never sport. How did this happen when I explicitly asked life's barber to cut it differently, to avoid the resemblance? It wasn't that I didn't appreciate my parents; I simply did not want to turn out like them.

I tried to get the attention of the bartender, who looked vaguely familiar, but he was engaged in a conversation with the only other person at the counter. The El Tovar Lounge had a distinctively different feel than the rustic lobby: Exposed pine beams were replaced by dark oak paneled walls and ceilings, warm wood floors were replaced by stain-forgiving red carpet, and craftsman furniture pieces were replaced by basic cocktail tables and chairs. If it were not for the large picture window exposing the canyon, it could have been an anywhere dive bar. The darkness masked whether the fog still loitered outside. Dimly lit by wall sconces and thick with smoke, the lounge had a dozen patrons. Lynyrd Skynyrd kept asking *what's your name* from an overhead speaker. Though my first visit to this lounge nearly ended my life after only twenty-two years, it thankfully also merged me with Mae for the next twenty-two. How Mae and I met was such a great story. It was the type of story that should always have a happy ending—not a premature one. Wouldn't the upcoming third twenty-two-year chapter in my life story be the perfect time to resolve any conflicts created in the second chapter? Isn't that why George Lucas planned two *Star Wars* sequels, not one?

The bartender, *Tom* per nametag, took notice of me and, when we made eye contact, there was a faint recognition and momentary pause while our brains unsuccessfully tried to establish why. He was a tall, heavyset Native American, a little older than I, with a ponytail and severely pockmarked cheeks. After pouring me a Lite, he returned to his discussion with the other barfly, who I now realized also looked familiar.

"Journey with Steve Perry or Gregg Rolie on vocals?" the other guy asked Tom.

"Steve Perry, hands down," Tom said.

"Have you ever heard 'Feeling That Way' where they share lead vocals?" I interrupted them.

"That song is Dyn-o-mite! I listened to the *Infinity* album just yesterday," Tom said.

I could not believe the overused JJ Walker catchphrase remained in circulation.

The other guy reached over to shake my hand, "I'm Willie. Nice to meet you." Willie was tipsy.

"Kevin," I said, as we shook. "What are you guys talking about?"

"Seventies rock songs you like to shout out loud," Tom said.

"Anybody say 'Feels Like the First Time'?" I asked.

"We've already exhausted Foreigner," Willie said.

"What about Sweet's 'Fox on the Run?'" I asked.

"We said Sweet's 'Ballroom Blitz.' How does 'Fox' go again?" Tom asked.

Willie boldly launched into the first line, *I don't wanna know your name.*

"Dyn-o-mite."

Some guy held up cash between Willie and me and asked Tom for a beer.

"Sit on it, Potsie! I'm busy," Tom said. The guy turned away, confused.

"What about 'Free Ride' by Edgar Winter?" Willie said, and pointed excitedly at both of us. "Or that one by Foghat?"

"'Slow Ride,'" Tom and I shouted back in unison.

"Didn't you have a band for a while?" Tom asked Willie.

"Yeah. Willie Aames and Paradise," Willie said. "We weren't as good as we thought we were."

I knew the name Willie Aames from somewhere. I looked at my fellow tippler/seventies rock enthusiast more carefully. The name and face registered.

"You played Tommy on *Eight Is Enough*," I said.

"Back in the day," he said.

I offered to buy Willie Aames a beer and he eagerly accepted. I asked him what he had acted in lately and he named a few projects I had not heard of—to his disappointment. He was at the Grand Canyon recording the narration for a new visitor center documentary.

The three of us continued our journey through the seventies charts, which included an excess of Miller Lite to jog our memories, until Tom had to close up at eleven. He let Willie Aames and me remain at the bar while he kicked everyone else out. Mae was not going to appreciate how long it was taking for *a* drink.

"Willie, there's something I have to ask," I said.

"No. I never slept with any of the actresses who played my sisters."

"How did you know I was going to ask that?"

"Everybody does."

"I saved the best for last," Tom said. From behind the bar he pulled out a black Sanyo radio and cassette player. It looked similar to the one my best friend used to own. He popped in a tape, intentionally blocking the artist name from Willie Aames and me.

I instantly recognized the opening guitar riff and drum beat of Jay Ferguson's "Thunder Island" and nodded my appreciation to Tom. Willie Aames affirmed his opinion by jumping off the stool and jamming on his air guitar. Willie Aames was *really* short. We all looked at each other to see if we were in agreement on who would take the lead. Ironically, my wife, who was upstairs enjoying her quiet evening, taught me to sing boldly and unabashedly in public.

Willie and I shared lead vocals on the first line, *sha-la-la-la-la-la my lady | in the sun with your hair undone.* I would not step down. I wanted to control this. I wanted to control *something.* Willie Aames, I'll whack you on the head with my *wasn't-meant-to-be* crutch if you don't back down. I outsang him on the next, *can you hear me now calling your name | from across the bay.* He reluctantly yielded and I finished out the first verse, *a summer's day laughing and a-hidin' | chasing love out on Thunder Island.*

We all engaged in the chorus, and Tom turned the bar counter into an air piano. As Willie Aames strummed his air guitar, I could see the disappointment in his face. I guiltily handed him the reins for the second verse. A long air guitar and air piano instrumental followed, and then all three of us united for the final verse and some chorus repeats, and I added in a show-stopping spoon to draft glass cowbell. I felt incredible and, for the first time in a long while, not vulnerable.

I stumbled up the stairs to our room and fumbled loudly with the key. Mae was asleep, lying with her back to me. I tiptoed in, stripped down to my underwear, and carefully pulled the sheets back. When I got in, I heard her quietly whimpering. Oh, shit. *I* should not have stayed out so late when this trip was patently for *us*. I spooned to her back and draped my arm over her. At first there was no response, which made me feel worse. Then she grabbed my arm and held it tight while pushing her body back to mold with mine. All was good.

9. '79

"Anne's in trouble," Mae said between deep breaths when she reached us.

We ran, towing Chad, towards the bridge where she came from. She said Anne was acting delirious, likely severely dehydrated, and their canteens were empty. Along the way I enlightened her on my new role as reluctant babysitter to a magic trail mix–eating singer.

"She's gone," Mae said in a panic when we reached the bridge entrance. "I left her over there." She pointed to a nearby spot in the deep trail sand where her pack and a large butt imprint remained.

We spun around, scanning the area. Chad's eyes widened as his head turned faster than he could track. We looked gravely at the river and froze. Back where the Bright Angel trail became the River trail, there had been a warning sign: *Colorado River, Dangerous current, Swimming not permitted.* If Anne had attempted a sip from the river and fallen in, there was no way she would have survived in her weakened and confused state.

"Over there!" Mae shouted. She pointed towards the center span of the steel bridge, one hundred and fifty feet away, where the bottom of the suspension cable met the four-foot-high hand railing in the center.

Anne was climbing up onto the railing. It was too far to shout with the competing river rumble. The bridge span was not wide enough for comfortable side-by-side crossing so I took the lead, tugging Chad behind me onto the see-through metal grate deck, with Mae trailing. With thirty-five feet of nothing between my hiking boots and the rushing water, feelings from the morning's near-death fall assaulted me. It was perfectly safe, with the grating and the side fencing, yet, as I earlier felt the magnetic pull from the canyon, I felt a similar inexorable pull from the river. It was an overwhelmingly insecure feeling. Chewbacca freaked out as soon as his paws stepped over the void. He halted and practically pulled my arm out of its socket. Looking out at Anne, standing fully upright on the railing and hanging on to one of the suspenders, I knew time was of the essence.

"Hold this," I shouted to Mae, and handed over Chad's hand. The transition was seamless and he did not protest. While they remained, I sprinted across the deck, adrenaline beating back insecurity.

Anne bent her knees and there was no doubt what her intentions were.

"Stop!" I yelled.

Her head turned towards me, but her knees remained flexed and ready to take the plunge. She would survive the fall, impact, and submergence into the deep Colorado, but with her clouded thinking she would have no chance against the frigid temperature, strong undertow, and chaotic rapids. Also, the fact that her pack was still mounted to her body was a critically poor decision.

"I have water!" I yelled, and outstretched my canteen as temptation. I stopped ten feet away, being careful not to startle her over the edge.

"Thanks," she said. "I'm going to get in a quick workout. I'll get some after I swim to shore."

"You realize swimming in the river is illegal because it's so dangerous," I said.

"Man, you probably can see I'm more capable than most," she said.

I concluded this situation was not going to be resolved with logic. I contemplated lunging forward to grab a hold of a leg, but her one step/fall would unquestionably take less time than my few to reach her. As she flexed her knees further, an alternate plan formed in my head, and I had no time to evaluate its worth.

"Kurt Russell needs your help," I said.

"What?" She stopped moving.

"Kurt Russell needs your help crossing the bridge. He's scared of heights." I was glad I was out of Mae's earshot so I could give the line my thespian best without cracking.

"Where is he?" she asked.

"Over there," I pointed at Chad one hundred and fifty feet away. I suppose he *sort of* looked like Kurt Russell, in a Borg kind of way.

Anne's eyes narrowed as she gazed in his direction. "I'll help Kurt," she said proudly, and jumped off the railing onto the deck, sending a shockwave through the flexible steel structure that threw me against the railing.

As I led Anne back to the others she casually drank from my canteen, as if it had nothing to do with how we got to this point. In the distance I could see Chad's free hand death-gripping the railing, his head bowed and eyes closed. Mae smiled at my conquest, but I grasped there were *two* birds I needed to kill, and my mind was trying to find the *one* stone. When we reached them, I positioned Anne next to Chad and paused. I tried to focus on anything besides what was about to come out of my mouth or else laughter would disable my speech.

"I'd like you to meet Kurt Russell," I said to Anne and gestured to Chad. Mae looked at me in disbelief, and then looked at Anne's acceptance in disbelief. Chad didn't look up, open his eyes, or even flinch.

"He's shy," I said. I leaned towards Chad and whispered into his ear, "This is the stripper I hired for you." His eyes shot open. Mae overheard and punched me in the arm.

"Kurt, I'd like you to meet Shotput Annie," I said. "She'd like to walk you to Phantom Ranch. Okay?" Anne extended her hand out and Chad ditched Mae's and grabbed it.

"Shotput Annie," Anne said to no one in particular. "I like it!"

"You know? You look a lot different in person," Anne said to Chad. "Shorter, with longer hair. And I wouldn't have pegged you as the headband type."

Chad's eyes were all over the place trying to take in all of Anne. Who knew what he was thinking.

"He's trying to get into character for his next role, the Björn Borg story," Mae said.

I choked on a laugh. Playing make-believe was always more fun with others.

"But Borg is alive," Anne said.

"It's called Björn Borg, the early years," I clarified. "It focuses on his difficult decision choosing between a professional tennis career or joining his good friend Björn Ulvaeus in ABBA."

"Right on," Anne said. She began pulling Chad, who now sported a sinister grin, across the bridge. "Come on, Kurt, you'll be okay."

I helped Mae put her pack back on, shared some water, and then we followed closely behind Kurt Russell and Shotput Annie. After crossing the Colorado, we crossed another short, controversy-free bridge over Bright Angel Creek, which flowed through both Phantom Ranch and the Bright Angel Campground before dumping into the Colorado. We turned up creek into a valley rich in greenery like Indian Garden. When we reached the crowded Bright Angel Campground, the girls' accommodations,

Mae conceded it made sense to hydrate and rest Anne out of the sun in our nearby Phantom Ranch cabin. Walking closely, side-by-side, my eyes collected additional subtleties of Mae: baby freckles perched on her nose, cheek tops, shoulders, and forearms; a dull pencil tip–shaped scar on the side of her chin; a fine blanket of translucent blonde hair rested on the back of her neck; a trace of extra length and thickness in her eyelashes wrestled my gaze from her dimples with each flutter.

Chad had remained mute, but his smile grew obnoxiously large. Anne, who had been thrilled Kurt Russell wanted to continue holding her hand after the suspension bridge, was also content in the silence. I felt conflicted, fearing she was drinking Kurt Russell away with each sip of water she took. Her only comment had been a question about whether ABBA would have had to change their band name if Björn Borg had joined them, since each letter represented a member's first initial. Mae handled the question like a pro, saying they would have added another *B* in the middle and the pronunciation of ABBBA would have remained the same.

We arrived at Phantom Ranch and concluded our weird and dangerous, yet entertaining and promising, half-day hike. We passed a mule corral, ranger station, amphitheater, a dozen cabins, restrooms, showers, and ended at the canteen, which housed the store, dining hall, and check-in desk. All of the earth-toned stone buildings blended naturally into the setting. Guests were littered about in stress-free poses. Densely planted cottonwood trees kept much of the ranch shaded.

A very nice older couple, who appeared to be a park ranger and his wife, welcomed us outside the canteen. They looked like thinner versions of Archie and Edith Bunker. Ranger Carroll sported a military style buzz cut and wore a weathered ranger's uniform, and his wife, Jeanne, wore simple khaki shorts and a t-shirt. They agreed to watch our disheveled kids outside while Mae and I checked in.

Inside, two rangers not much older than us were playing the new *Electronic Battleship* at the front desk. As they stood to greet us, I released a *wow* instead of a standard check-in pleasantry. They were dead ringers for Officers Jon Baker and Frank Poncherello, a.k.a. *Ponch*, from the show *CHiPs*.

"Yes, we know. You don't need to say it," the blond-haired ranger said.

"It's uncanny," I said.

"We hear it way too much. Are you checking in?" the dark-haired Hispanic ranger said.

"Is this a hybrid California Highway Patrol and National Park Ranger position?" I asked.

"Did Sergeant Getraer warn you about us during today's roll call briefing?" Mae asked.

"Very funny," said the now pissed off blond. "You know, we were partners well before Officers Baker and Poncherello were riding their motorcycles, disco dancing, and picking up chicks. We don't look like them; they look like us. Why should we break up a perfectly good partnership because of a shitty television show that will probably be cancelled soon anyways?" They both looked to be on the verge of tears.

"Only kidding, guys," I said.

"We're sorry," Mae said. She gave them a big, dimple-filled, lash-fluttering, disarming smile, diffusing an obviously sensitive topic.

We showed our reservation receipt, and I asked if they could do me a solid and let the girls stay in our cabin since Anne wasn't feeling well.

"It's okay by me," the Hispanic said with a grin. "The cabin has two sets of bunks, so do what comes naturally. But if he's not treating you with respect," he said to Mae, "you know where to find me."

I withheld a *fuck you, Ponch* comment.

The blond handed us the keys to cabin number eleven and gave us a meal schedule flyer. I thanked him and asked their names.

"I'm Ranger *blah*," the blond said.

"I'm Ranger *blah*," the Hispanic said. My mind censored both responses since it was already locked on Baker and Ponch.

"Were you by chance in Indian Garden earlier?" the Hispanic asked.

"Yes. Why?" Mae asked.

"Did you see the two fruits prancing around, holding hands, and singing songs from *Grease*? I heard it was hilarious." There was a walkie-talkie on their table.

"They weren't prancing," I said defensively. "They were hiking. And only *one* guy sang *one* song. It was out of the ordinary, but not hilarious."

Mae transitioned my defense to her offense, "Don't you rangers have anything better to do than make fun of people who are different than you? And who's to say what goes on between you two living in this remote location? You seem to be overcompensating something with this macho sexist act of yours."

"Sorry for my partner, ma'am. Have a safe stay," Baker said.

"Yes, sorry, ma'am," Ponch said.

Mae burst out laughing when we got outside. After making sure Kurt Russell and Shotput Annie went to the bathroom and chugged water from our newly refilled canteens, we headed to cabin number eleven, one of the four original cabins built in 1922. Consistent with most of the historic Phantom Ranch buildings, it was designed by Mary Jane Colter, who was also the architect for many of the defining south rim buildings. The walls were natural rock with larger boulders at the base, held together by thick mortar joints. It had a low-pitched, gabled, dark wood roof, and plant green exterior trim. It blended so well with the surroundings that it looked like it grew there. Once inside, Chad attempted to put a new tape into his stereo so Shotput Annie could start dancing. I interrupted him and calmly explained she was tired and needed to rest up for the evening's performance. It was warm inside, but tolerable for an afternoon siesta. Both Kurt and Shotput eagerly crawled into the bottom bunks of the two sets and gave in to their exhaustion. Mae and I, two people who did not know each other, were left in a quiet room of awkwardness.

It occurred to me how timely it was to be someplace as unique, beautiful, and historic as the bottom of the Grand Canyon in the healthy, optimistic, and unjaded soul of a youth with no job, exams, or anything coming remotely close to a responsibility, with an amusing, intriguing, and attractive girl to hang out with and a wide-open afternoon to exercise, philosophize, or extemporize. I was a fresh California State University graduate ready to prove my fully educated decision–making ability, and new goal-oriented attitude, to the adult community I was proudly now an accountable member of—*wanna get drunk?*

10. '79

The shiny white cans of the Miller Lite six-pack, anchored in a shallow part of the creek, reflected the sunlight and looked like an underwater fire. We sat on rocks with our bare feet in the cool water. With the burden of my pack gone, and the heavy claustrophobic hiking boots replaced by sandals, I felt like I would float away at any moment. We watched a helicopter trace Bright Angel Creek in the sky.

"So, you're well-read," Mae said.

"What makes you think so?" I asked.

"At the first resthouse, you attempted a Vonnegut *Breakfast of Champions* reference with your *Bermuda Ern* comment. Then at the second resthouse you referred to our discussion as a *Chautauqua*, which is from Pirsig's *Zen and the Art of Motorcycle Maintenance*. You were reaching with both of those, you know?"

I smiled at her recognition. Other avid recreational readers in college had been rare to find.

She continued, "Next time for a Vonnegut reference, use *so it goes* from *Slaughterhouse-Five*."

"I'm impressed," I said.

"Well, I like escapism, and books are a safer choice than drugs. Except for *The Anarchist Cookbook*."

Mae selflessly saved a Lite can from drowning.

"It's not going to be cold enough," I said.

"If I needed cold I'd drink the creek water."

"Good point," I said, and grabbed a can.

"Want to play bocce ball?" I asked.

"You'll have to teach me how."

I felt around in the water and fished out seven stones: one cherry-sized brown one, three lighter-shaded racquetball-sized, and three darker racquetball-sized. We got out of the creek bed and I tossed the smaller rock, the *jack*, thirty feet away near a cottonwood trunk. I handed her the three lighter-shaded rocks and explained we would alternate throws and the object was to toss as close to the jack as possible; the player with the nearest rock, or rocks, received one point for each; first one to ten won.

While I tossed the inaugural, she revived our literature Chautauqua, "So, like *Breakfast* and *Zen*, are you a little bit crazy *and* deep?"

"Crazy? No. Deep? I'm not sure."

Mae removed her straw hat and let it hang on her back by its cord, then lobbed her first rock. It was an awkward, not athletically conditioned motion.

I added, "I overthink everything so I could be deep, though I think about a lot of different things so I might be wide, not deep, or just neurotic. You?" My Lite was already warm and accelerated consumption was necessary.

"I've got a little crazy in me, and I think depth is in the eye of the beholder," she said. "The reason Anne and I are best friends is because I appreciate and embrace originality, while most people are confused and worried by it. Are you a rationalist or romanticist?"

I considered her question from *Zen* while we each finished delivering our final two rocks. "More rationalist, but I've got some romanticist in me. I think you need both, but leaning too hard in one direction can be dangerous. How about you?"

"I tend to romanticize more than rationalize," she said. "Thinking scares me because I'm always afraid I'll make the wrong decision. If I act first, think second, I don't have a choice."

We walked over to our rocks and the jack. I did not appreciate how hot it was until I entered the welcoming shade of the cottonwood. All three of Mae's rocks were closer to the jack than any of mine—beginner's luck.

"Three points to you," I said, "and winner throws the jack."

She lightly rolled the jack underneath a picnic table twenty feet away, scaring off an unsuspecting chipmunk.

"Whose story would you want to live?" I asked and then released my first rock with a low trajectory.

"What?"

"What characters appeal to you?"

"Interesting question because there seem to be two extremes for women," she said. "*The Total Woman* says women should worship their husbands and wrap themselves naked in saran wrap to welcome them home from work. And *The Stepford Wives* are submissive, docile robots. On the other hand, in *Looking for Mr. Goodbar*, Theresa Dunn sought one night stands of violent sex, and in *The Fear of Flying*, Isadora Wing sought emotionless sex with strangers, which she called *zipless fucks*."

"There's got to be middle ground between robot wives and *zipless fucks*," I suggested.

"There's Britta, Monica, and Gretchen, the female runaways in *The Drifters*. They were young and free and had wild experiences in exotic places, but one of them overdosed on heroin. So, if the author's not going to make you a slut, they're going to get you addicted to drugs."

"What about *Carrie?*" I asked sarcastically.

"My brother really liked that book," she said. "He was bullied in high school and he appreciated how she got revenge."

"He appreciated her locking the students in the school, setting it on fire, and blowing it up?" I asked.

"Well, he appreciated the concept, at least."

She released her last rock and added, "Jenny Cavilleri was a strong character."

"Jenny was great," I said. Everybody mourned Jenny's passing in the novel, then movie, *Love Story*.

"I guess a strong *and* loving woman makes for a boring story since the author had to kill her off," she said.

"What did you think of the second book?"

"*Oliver's Story* sucked. By the very definition of true love, you cannot have a *Love Story* part two."

"You think there's only one person out there for you?"

She paused while we assessed our points from round two: two for me. "I guess not. But I do know that when I find the first one of them, I'm giving my all like Jenny did."

We retrieved two much cooler Lites from the creek. I pitched the jack fifty feet across a meadow, where it settled next to a round, blue-green agave plant with a phallic, twelve-foot-high yellow seed stalk.

Mae readied to give her rock a good heave. "It's funny. Out of all of the characters out there, I guess I most relate to a male seagull."

"*Jonathan Livingston?*" I guessed.

"Yeah. My life has no room for conformity, and I have an intense passion for motion and personal growth, like his passion for flight."

"Interesting," I said. "Especially since I can most relate to a rabbit."

"Hey, I was taking this discussion seriously."

"I'm totally serious," I said. "Fiver from *Watership Down*. He's a seer. He had the vision of his warren's destruction and knew they needed to seek a new home." I hesitated before an uncomfortable admission. "Like him, I think I sometimes get glimpses of things before they happen. And we're both quiet, but intelligent."

"Glimpses? Do you have the *shine*?" she asked as I threw my rock at the floral genitalia.

I smiled at her reference to Danny Torrance's psychic abilities in *The Shining*, the most uncomfortable book I had ever read. The topic of having visions was embarrassing for me because even though I thought I did, I had no way to prove it. I would have shared less if I were not in a remote location with a stranger.

"Call it whatever you want, but I sometimes see things," I said. "They don't always come true, but some do."

She looked at me skeptically. "I believe you."

The awkwardness of the topic dissipated. It was nice when someone appreciated you putting yourself out there, instead of trying to bring you down.

After we released our last rocks, she asked, "Wasn't it also a burden for Fiver when he saw terrible events in advance and they came true? Didn't he blame himself?"

"Yes, and yes," I said. "It's a gift *and* a burden. There are many things you don't want to see, especially if they come true." I could see my response emotionally wounded her.

We walked over and assessed whose rocks were nearest to the aroused succulent. I picked up another point.

"It's damn hot out here," she said. Beads of sweat magnified the freckles on her nose. "Do you mind if we call it a draw?"

We retrieved our last two chilled beers from the creek and grabbed another six-pack from the cabin. Kurt Russell and Shotput Annie were still knocked out. Chad would be pissed none of the first twelve aluminum cans had his fingerprints. We each drank our third as we walked over to the canteen to get out of the sun.

"Have you read *Ordinary People*?" she asked. Apparently, she felt compelled to delve deeper into the topic of personal burdens. I noticed an immediate change in her. She slowed, her shoulders slumped forward, and her head angled down.

"That was an incredibly sad story," I said. "I don't think I've ever pulled harder for anybody than Conrad. After his brother's accidental death he suffered from severe post-trauma stress *and* survivor's guilt *and* he attempted suicide."

"What saddened me the most," Mae said, "was how so many people wanted him to act normal after all of that, because it would make them feel more comfortable. Why do humans always think of themselves first?"

"I never thought of that," I said.

"Have you read *What Dreams May Come?*" she asked.

"No. What's it about?" I asked.

"The husband dies in an accident," she said, "and then the grieving wife commits suicide. He goes to heaven, but she goes to hell because she took her own life. Do you think it's wrong for someone to choose to end his or her life to escape a deep physical or emotional pain?"

"I don't have an answer to a question like that," I said. I wanted to lighten a conversation that somehow turned dark. "Mae, *I'm OK, You're OK.*"

"Hah!" she mocked. "That one started *it* all."

"Started *what?*"

"Some of the best sellers in the sixties were cookbooks and home fix-it manuals. In the seventies, those were replaced by diet and self-help books."

"I guess Americans got too fat and handy," I said.

She laughed. "They got lazy. Looking to others to tell them the right way to live their lives instead of figuring it out for themselves. It's sad. There's a lot of money to be made off laziness."

The canteen was empty mid-afternoon except for the kitchen staff. We each grabbed another Lite, Mae charmed one of the cooks into putting the remaining four-pack in the refrigerator, and she and I sat down at one of the community tables.

"Board game?" she asked.

"Right on," I said. Due to limited exposure in my youth, I was now a big fan of these, playing a lot in the fraternity house, usually with drinking rules incorporated.

She got up and scanned the titles with her back to me. Taking a journey from her cutoff Calvins to buffalo toe loop sandals, my eyes noted her shapely legs were not muscular—interests fell outside of athletics. She grabbed a handful of the boxes, stacked them on the table, dimpled her cheeks, and said, "This is what's wrong with our fucking society."

"What's wrong with our fucking society?" I repeated and clasped my hands behind my head. I could tell I was about to get passionate, alcohol-fueled lecturing; the key points forgotten by tomorrow.

She grabbed the top box and made a reverse pile. "*Pay Day, Billionaire, Prize Property, Monopoly, King Oil.*" She opened *King Oil.* "Object of the game: each player buys properties, drills for oil, invests his profits, installs pipelines, and collects royalties to become so powerful that he becomes *King Oil* and wins."

She opened the next one and continued, "*Monopoly.* Object: to become the wealthiest player through buying, renting, and selling of property.

"*Prize Property.* A game of land development and litigation. Be the first to build all of your nine buildings.

"*Billionaire.* Become a billionaire by investing in commodities around the world.

"*Pay Day.* To have the most money at the end of the game."

"I mean, seriously?" she said. "This is our form of escapism? This is what we fantasize about? To be *King fucking Oil?*"

I don't think she realized how much I was enjoying her at this point. I would have bought tickets for this.

She continued, "The more money my parents made, the more problems it created."

"Why don't we play something a little deeper?" I said, and pointed to the box of *Life* on the shelf.

"Oh, this should be interesting." She excitedly took it down, opened it up, and read, "The game ends when the last player goes bankrupt or becomes a millionaire."

"Count your money," she shouted, "the player with the most wins the game!" She sat down on the bench and took a long draw of her beer.

"I won't let all this commercialism ruin my Christmas," I said.

"Did you quote Charlie Brown? Seriously?"

"I'm weird like that," I said. "You know, *Life* was different when Milton Bradley invented it in the 1800s." It had been a discussion topic in my *Social Values* class last semester. "Although you were rewarded for good financial decisions, it was more about virtues versus vices. Board squares said things like *Honesty, Perseverance, Ruin, Prison,* and even *Suicide*, which showed a man hung from a tree. Simple rules: Land on a virtue and advance; land on a vice and it slows you down. You won by reaching a square called *Happy Old Age*."

Mae stared at me vacantly. "What's *Happy Old Age* like?"

"I suppose it's feeling happy because of all of your good choices in life."

Such a simple theory seemed to deeply impact Mae. "I like that. I *really* like that," she said.

She grinned. "You want to play a *Battleship* drinking game?"

"Who wouldn't?"

We pulled the *Electronic Battleship* box from the shelf. There were no instructions and we were both too buzzed to figure out how the electronic part worked, so we turned it off and played the old-fashioned way. Mae pontificated that you drink when you fire an errant missile, and when one of your boats gets hit. She was making this up as she went, but I was game.

"And no moving your ships during the game," she said.

"Why would I?"

"Because *everyone* does."

I thought back to my pitiful *Battleship* win/loss record. "Crap!"

Fifteen minutes later, while finishing the last of our beers, Mae interrupted our limited *miss, hit,* and *sunk* conversation, "Let's write the object of the game for *our* lives."

"What do you mean?"

"Object of the game, or how to win, at life. One line." She rose unsteadily, pulled a *Boggle* box off the shelf, and pilfered two pieces of paper and pencils.

While I meditated on the assignment, I noticed Mae was struggling, crossing out multiple false starts. I glanced at her paper and saw verbs: *travel, explore,* and *experience,* that did not make the cut. I considered using something from the Bible, but opted to write the first Kevin verse that came to mind. I wrote it out in one attempt and saw no need to edit. I looked up to see how Mae was progressing and discovered she was asleep on the table, head resting on folded arms. Her paper was sticking halfway out under a hand, and I tentatively snuck the cheese out of the mousetrap. She had completed her one line, and while trying to focus my eyes to read it, I drifted off.

The smack of a plastic tray on the community table awoke Goldilocks and me. We were sandwiched elbow-to-elbow amongst the canteen's five-thirty dinner crowd. Multilingual conversations surrounded us, and the air was thick with smoke. Baker and Ponch made the rounds, with Baker answering questions while Ponch fished with pickup lines. Ranger Carroll and his wife were eating with the guests. She was extremely motherly, tucking a napkin into his shirt, bib style, and cutting up his steak for him.

A highly elastic thread of spit anchored Mae's yawning mouth to the table. Instead of the steak or stew options, we were apparently the only diners who ordered the warship sampler plate. Groggy and buzzed, Mae looked around for her *object of the game* note. My last vague memory was an attempt to read hers, but now I did not see it anywhere. Mine was also missing. Neither of us could remember what we wrote.

Mae and I both opted for the beef stew and then became immersed in conversations with travelers from all over the world. Most everyone had been kissed by the sun and donned a blessed look, as if Phantom Ranch at the bottom of the Grand Canyon had chosen them, and not vice versa. Next to us were a French brother and sister, about our age, who were backpacking across the U.S. She was pretty, fair-skinned with blue eyes and heavy dark eyebrows. I did not pay any attention to what he looked like. When Mae and I mentioned we just met today, the sister angled her body towards mine and became much more animated with her clichéd accent. Mae picked up on the vibe change and coupled her own speech with hand gestures, grabbing my arms during the italics of her stories. Marlin Perkins of *Wild Kingdom* was providing commentary in my head. When Mae mentioned we needed to go check on our friends and grabbed both my arms across the tabletop, I took the hint. I felt the foreign blue eyes track my departure.

You would think the canteen was on fire based on how much smoke poured out the windows. The warm summer night air, combined with a soft breeze rustling the cottonwood leaves and the steady babble of Bright Angel Creek, made it feel like nature had calculatingly staged our walk back to the cabin. The western canyon wall cast an earlier than expected evening shading, though the top of the eastern wall remained lit up like a blazing orange match head. As we strolled to the cabin, a swift clomping of hiking boots caused us to stop and turn around. The French girl was jogging after us.

"Seriously?" Mae whispered.

"I think this is yours," the accent said when she caught us. She held out a piece of paper.

"What is it?" I asked.

She read it, "Kevin's object of the game: Make others realize they're not alone." With a French narration my three-hour-old drunken thought sounded so much more meaningful. I took it, thanked her, and she lingered a moment to see if I would offer her more than a verbal gratitude. Awkward. A *g'night* and half wave clued her to retreat.

I resumed walking with Mae, who had remained quiet during the exchange. A few steps later, she grabbed my hand and stopped us. She was smiling but had a single tear on her left cheek. It was a difficult face to read and I was unsure what would follow. She guided me backwards a few steps, up against a cottonwood trunk, clasped her hands behind my neck, and craned up for a long, drawn-out kiss. At first she was trembling, clearly not from the warm evening, more from somewhere inside, and I responded with comforting touches, which steadied her and strengthened the kiss.

Although it was the perfect ending to my first, and probably last, games-themed date, it was short-lived. We were interrupted by a déjà vu chorus, this time without Chad accompanying Dionne Warwick, of *I know I'll never love this way again.*

"Could that be coming from our cabin?" Mae disengaged and asked.

I remembered the original purpose of *Tender Chad*, which was not to calm someone hiking along sheer vertical drops.

"Oh, shit!"

In the distance, we saw Chad stumble out the front door of cabin number eleven. He paused, looked both ways without noticing us, dropped his OPs to his knees and pissed. I smiled knowing what came next. Chad guided his aim with his hand and pretended to slash Stormtroopers with his steaming stream, accompanied by varying intensities of humming. Mae stifled her laughter to avoid disrupting his playtime. When he had slayed enough of the Imperial Army, he pulled his OPs up and staggered in our direction. His clothes and hair were unkempt, his cheeks were flushed, and he wore his headband around his neck like a collar. Mae took a few steps back from me so no previous activity was obvious.

His eyes lit up when he noticed us. "Are they still serving?" he asked. "I'm starving." He smelled like *Wild Kingdom.*

"Yes. Are you feeling okay now?" I asked.

"Yeah. I'm copacetic."

"Is that your tape playing?"

"Yeah. I'm a little fuzzy on how long it's been going or who turned it on. To be honest, I'm not sure what happened back there. I heard so many different names being said that I thought it was an orgy. There was skin everywhere and I'm not sure the right parts were even going in the right places, though I think every fluid in my body has been depleted. I've gotta refuel. Catch you on the flip side." He swayed on towards the canteen.

Mae yelled after him, "Is Anne okay?"

"She fell back asleep," he shouted over his shoulder. A few seconds later, "Might not want to touch either of the bottom bunks." Another few seconds later, "Also, might want to open a window or door for a while."

DAY 2

11. '01

S he was gone when I woke. My first, anxious thought was that she impulsively left me for good while I slept off my concert hangover. My second was that I had extinguished the impulsive side of Mae many times over. Was she still capable of unpredictability? Her purse and the car keys were on the nightstand—safe—for now. Scribbled on the hotel notepad was: *Bright Angel Coffee.*

As I threw on jeans and my gray SDSU hooded sweatshirt, I observed how little the morning light impacted the room. Looking out the window, aside from the exterior of the hotel, everything was still grayed out. Seeing this at eight in the morning gave me confidence it could burn off as the day progressed. Growing up in San Diego, I developed a sixth sense for where and when the coastal marine layer would dissipate.

Sipping a mug of coffee in the middle of the generously sized Bright Angel Restaurant, Mae was peering upwards and deep in thought when I arrived. She had bags under her slightly bloodshot eyes, and I assumed she had been crying again. The depression from the plausible divorce was unbearable for both of us. Mae, who always felt strongly about dealing head on with despair, let it saturate her and spill over at will. For me, just like with the unknown, I practiced ignorance and avoidance in an attempt to distort and escape reality. Although even my strongest shield kept cracking under the recent pressure, resulting in private moments of full body sobbing that I pridefully tried to conceal.

Based on the crowd, bad weather was great for sausage and pancake sales. Before approaching Mae, I looked upwards to confirm whether her focus was outward, or vacant with inward thoughts. There was nothing to note on the high wood-beamed ceiling. My kiss on her cheek snapped her back.

"Why didn't you wake me?" I asked.

"I don't know. I wanted a little time."

Was time with me *wasted* time?

"Have you ordered?" I asked.

"No. I was waiting for you."

After our waitress took our order, Mae's astray eyes connected with mine and I knew a discussion, *the* discussion, was about to commence.

"I need to share what's been weighing on my heart," she said, "and let's not forget to call Warren after breakfast."

We had opted for the undisturbed canyon trip instead of driving north to Westmont College in Montecito to celebrate our youngest's nineteenth birthday. I had felt I could successfully mesh a celebration with marriage reconciliation; Mae had not. It was the first birthday of Warren's life we spent apart. I knew he was okay with it, but I felt a void. My need to feel close with our kids instinctually intensified once I grasped how endangered our marriage had become. With both kids now out of the house in college, I felt like an anchorless dinghy in rough waters.

"Honey, it's his birthday," I said. "Let's call him now while it's early."

"He can wait. He's probably sleeping."

"Nonsense. He's up and waiting for our call. Let's call."

"You go ahead. I'll call him later," she said coolly.

I hesitantly got up and walked over to the Bright Angel lobby to use a phone. I could feel her eyes and thoughts through the back of my head and knew my recent fixed mindset of avoidance had just invoked further unnecessary damage. There was no answer in Warren's dorm room.

I had lobbied hard for an in-state school, like our daughter chose, which would make visits easier. Mae's preference was for more distance to promote independent thinking and self-awareness. *Less like me?* I also lobbied for a large school, similar to what Mae and I both attended. Mae preferred a smaller school, citing U of A had been rife with mob mentality distractions. I liked the familiar path while Mae liked to use past experiences to change the future.

Even though Westmont was a small liberal arts college, I was pleased with Warren's choice since it was only three hours away. Curiously, he did not come home once in his first semester. I drove up there on my own, against Mae's wishes, one weekend in October, and although he happily showed me around campus and introduced me to his friends on Friday, I could tell he was annoyed I planned to stay the whole weekend. I drove home Saturday morning with my tail between my legs.

The kids were young adults and well aware mom and dad had their struggles. Mae once said she thought kids learned more from their parents' behavior than from what they tried to teach them. I felt insufferable guilt knowing we might have taught them a lesson plan for failure. Had I failed at marriage *and* parenthood? Surely, Mae would do *anything* to avoid this. Right?

Mae was staring at the ceiling again when I returned. It felt silly greeting her with a kiss on the cheek for the second time in ten minutes, so I simply sat down and waited for her gaze to lower.

"You'd do anything for those kids," she said when she acknowledged me. It did not sound like a compliment.

"As would you."

"I suppose."

"Mae, what's on your mind?"

"I'm hungry. Let's eat first and talk later."

I knew her need for food was secondary to her need for a connection, and sensed this was an opportunity for me to passionately object and insist we work on *us*. Instead, I opted to accept her submission. After breakfast we walked west along the rim trail, past the Lookout and Kolb Studio. Our uninspired, halfhearted pace reflected our mood. Temperatures remained cool and my hands dove deep in my pockets while Mae retracted hers into the sleeves of a golden U of A fleece. We paused at the beginning of the Bright Angel trail—*our* beginning. She gave me a clowning push towards the edge and I feigned a plunge. It was clowning, *right?* We continued ten minutes farther to the Trailview Overlook, peering into the Bright Angel Fault, willing the fog to lift so we could at least see the upper portion of the trail.

At dinner parties, when couples asked us how we first met, our story never disappointed. It had all of the necessary components: depth, humor, passion, danger, twists, and cliffhangers (suspenseful *and* literal). And although it transpired over a brief period, three days, it was difficult to make it a short story. All details, complexities, and meaningful discussions were necessary to disclose, to solve why two very different individuals felt compelled to spend their lives together after just three days. Looking back now at Mae's and my *whole* story, the beginning was categorically the best part. I suppose that meant everything after was a bit of a letdown. So, would our story have best been unwritten?

Standing next to me, staring toward the invisible fault, Mae spotted something. Her eyes narrowed, then slowly widened, paired with a retracting of cheeks and deepening of dimples. As I stared into the fog and struggled to identify the source of her amusement, she reached for my left hand with her right. I obliged and she held it tightly between us. She kept smiling, but closed her eyes. She was looking *back*. You could not help it when you looked into the canyon, fog or not. The Kaibab limestone our sneakers rested on was 250 million years old. The rock layers at the bottom of the canyon were six times as ancient. Looking back was always the easy part. It devastated me how she was struggling to look forward.

12. '79

At breakfast, which the four of us gingerly walked our post-hike-stiffened legs over to, I witnessed the canteen's worst nightmare when a rapacious Anne partook of the *all-you-can-eat* breakfast buffet. I got my fill of bacon, eggs, and pancakes, but many guests who slept in would not. She and Chad chattered carefreely with us and the other guests, but no mention was made of yesterday's unusual series of events, including whatever might, or might not, have occurred in cabin number eleven; or the mysterious disappearances of Kurt Russell and Shotput Annie.

To my annoyance, the topic of last night's kiss, which clearly did occur, was also not revisited. And Mae acted no different this morning than she did prior to the event. I was not exactly sure what I expected her to say, but I felt some sort of acknowledgement was deserved. Moreover, I needed validation. I was once again insecurely reaching for my *wasn't-meant-to-be* crutch I had vowed to throw away. I tended to overanalyze and look for only obvious signs to understand where I stood in a situation and what my next move should be. I was more Potsie than Fonzie.

Chad and Anne remained at the canteen to ask around for daytime exploring ideas. Mae and I savored our Folgers on the front step of cabin number eleven. The top of the western canyon wall directly behind us was illuminated soft purple. It was the closest proximity we had been to each other since last night's encounter. After airing the cabin out, which was a requirement, not an elective, and forcing a half-naked Olympic shotputting hopeful to chug water, Mae and I ended last night by retiring in separate top bunks.

We quietly watched Ranger Carroll doing his morning rounds. He kept repeating a loop around the cabins, bathrooms, canteen, and dorms, stopping to answer questions whenever approached. Curiously, he always paused at an open field, dense with a surplus of large rocks, in front of the employee bunkhouse. He would pace around the field, reach down, let a handful of dirt sift through his fingers, and then scratch his head. Mae and I, playing amateur sociologists, could not postulate an explanation. Another observation we found interesting was how his wife always trailed closely behind him, not interfering with his job. I assumed she was a doting partner. Mae suggested she should be more independent. I argued it was none of our business what makes someone else happy—an opinion that angered her. Seeking a topic change, I asked her whom she wanted to work for when she graduated. Again, I unwittingly screwed up.

"*Nobody* is *whom* I want to work for," she said, agitated. "It's more about what I want to do, for myself."

"Okay, *what* work will you do for yourself, and *who* pays you for it?"

"I don't exactly know yet. Something dynamic. Not routine or stagnant. What were your plans again?"

"Working in my uncle's real estate office, to start." Halfway through saying it, I was afraid she would fall asleep. Sadly, I felt the same way.

Ranger Carroll looped in front of us. I called out to him to help resuscitate our tetchy conversation, "Ranger Carroll, do you like your job?" He walked over with his wife in tow.

"I couldn't be happier," he said. "I get to work in one of God's most beautiful creations, meet and help people from all over the world, and spend every day alongside the woman I love."

Jeanne's enormous smile warmed me.

"Whom do you work for?" Mae asked him.

"Well, the Grand Canyon is a National Park, so up until this past April, my boss was Franklin Roosevelt, rest in peace, but now I work for Harry S. Truman. You kids enjoy your stay at the ranch." He reentered his loop.

We both smiled, but I didn't get his joke about past presidents.

"Was he kidding?" I asked Mae.

She shrugged her shoulders. "Probably. I liked his job description, though." She got up and brushed dirt off the seat of her cutoffs.

"You've got to be fucking kidding me," Wolfman's voice carried across the ranch.

"I think Chad just met Baker and Ponch," I said.

A short while later, the four of us exited out the back end of Phantom Ranch on the North Kaibab trail, which connected to the north rim fourteen miles away. Chad accessorized his brown and yellow *Padres #31* jersey—Dave Winfield let him borrow it—with his Borg headband, a six-pack of Miller Lite, and his stereo—the stereo was included with his action figure. I donned an orange *Sunkist Good Vibrations* tee and a daypack for water. We both wore swim trunks and our striped Rainbow sandals. Anne complemented her cowboy hat and cutoffs with a harvest gold bikini top—sightseers on the canyon rims could likely spot it—and Dr. Scholl's exercise sandals. Mae donned her wide-brimmed hat and cutoffs, along with an avocado green bikini top and her buffalo toe loop sandals. I hoped the girls' bikini bottoms, caged in their cutoffs, would make an appearance.

"Where are you kids headed?" Ranger Carroll yelled at our backs. He was standing outside the hiker dormitories and his wife stood near him.

"One of the other rangers told us about the Phantom Creek waterfall and swimming hole," Chad answered.

Ranger Carroll took off his hat and looked to the sky. We all did the same, although we were not sure why.

"If you see *any* clouds, make sure you stay on high ground," he said.

"Sure thing. I dig," Chad said.

The sky was deep blue with not a cloud in sight.

Chad decided the Steve Miller Band's *Book of Dreams* tape was the ideal soundtrack for our sojourn to the swimming hole. He and Anne split the beers since Mae and I had already got the day-drunk craving out of our system. We followed the Bright Angel Creek basin into a box canyon with steep granite walls only forty feet apart. The stagnant heat felt like a newly paved Sears parking lot.

"Where in the fuck are you supposed to go if this thing ever floods?" Chad asked.

"I think that was Ranger Carroll's point," Mae said. "You're not supposed to hike here if there's any chance of serious rain. The ground is water-resistant and the runoff builds quickly."

The surrounding walls made it impossible to see any distant weather.

"It's kind of like hiking through a drain," I said.

"It's *exactly* like hiking through a drain," Mae said.

Chad and Anne rapidly imbibed their Lites and fervently debated whether women could rock or not. He acknowledged Janis Joplin absolutely rocked, but no female had taken the torch after her overdose. Anne ill-advisedly suggested disco divas Houston, Gaynor, and Summer, which Chad disqualified since the *temporary* fad of disco was independent of rock. He then dismissed her submission of Grace Slick of Jefferson Starship as a drunk, Patti Smith as too weird, the Runaways as only easy to look at before they imploded, and Debbie Harry as guilty of treason for straddling the rock/disco fence. The momentum shifted when Anne proposed Christine McVie and Stevie Nicks of Fleetwood Mac, which Chad concurred with and admitted he owned the *Rumours* album. She also scored with Ann Wilson of Heart since "Barracuda" was one of his favorite songs. And he promised he would check out Girlschool, a new British band Anne liked.

I envied how passionate Chad got when discussing topics like music. He was highly opinionated, but his thoughts flowed without insecurities, and people enjoyed engaging him. I was drawn to this when we first met, as five-year-old Indian Guides trading beads. Our friendship was sealed when we realized my conscientious beads complemented his gregarious ones. It was obvious Anne shared a similar colloquial gene. My main vernacular challenge was that my favorite topic was a polarizing one—my faith. More often it inspired avoidance *instead* of engagement. What people misunderstood was that I did not bring it up to preach and convert; I brought it up because I wanted to know how others coped with life. Who wouldn't? And, frankly, it was the one thing I consistently felt secure about. In my exposed early teens, my parents demonstrated—via a slow motion implosion—that love and relationships could be conditional and temporary, and I witnessed their faith weaken throughout. Without any siblings, the only immediate family member I could depend on for stability was myself. It compelled me to reinforce my foundation to make it less susceptible to attacks. Unfortunately, it had been impossible to stare directly into the sun setting on my parents without incurring some damage.

I opted to participate in the lighter topic. "What about Suzi Quatro?" I asked Chad and Anne.

"Who?" Anne asked.

I slapped my thigh twice with my right hand and aimed a finger gun at her.

"Oh yeah," Chad said excitedly, and bit his hand à la Lenny. "She's the chick who plays Leather Tuscadero on *Happy Days*. She's a decent singer. Kevin digs her."

"Is that true?" Mae asked. "You like the skintight leather look?"

"I don't *dis*like it," I said.

"So you want the cool girl, without being cool?"

"Basically."

"Has Kevin told you gals yet he was almost on *Joker's Wild* college week?" Chad said with the sole purpose of embarrassing me.

"Were you really?" Mae asked.

"Yeah, but he flunked the personality test," Chad said.

"I didn't flunk the personality test," I said.

"Yeah, you did," Chad said. "Kevin's got a headful of useless trivia, like the all-important Suzi Quatro is Leather Tuscadero factoid, and he nailed the written test the show mailed him. He got disqualified after driving up to Century City to meet with the producers."

"Is *that* a goal of yours, to get on a game show?" Mae asked me.

"No," I said. "Chad submitted the application without telling me. He thought I could win us some money for a spring break trip."

"I think that would have been far out," Anne said. "Although, I'd rather be on *Tic-Tac-Dough*. I can't wait until all of my friends can see me on TV in Moscow next summer."

I noticed a repeating pattern of Mae making fun of me. I assumed this was flirting but was having trouble measuring her. I sensed there were some complexities hidden beneath her strong-willed, and very beautiful, top layer. Her excitement for the future made me wonder why she was so eager to escape from the past. Why would she be so declaratively vocal about her independence and then react so appreciatively to my life goal of making others realize they're not alone? And, why would she spontaneously kiss me last night and then act like the backside of a magnet today?

In a freshman literature class I had to write my interpretation of a French play called *Waiting for Godot*, a vague story about two guys waiting for something. The professor liked my thoughts and awarded me an *A*. I had to reinterpret the same play in a junior year class for a different professor. I recycled my first paper, but this time my opinions were rudely autographed with a *D*. For me, it was a similar scenario with girls; I always felt like I was writing a paper without knowing the grading criteria. Courting would be so much easier if it were more like the classic Dick and Jane books: *Kevin meets Mae. Mae meets Kevin. Kevin likes Mae. Mae likes Kevin. Kevin feels like makin' love to Mae. Mae feels like makin' love to Kevin.*

After walking a long stretch where our surroundings remained the same scale, it was impossible not to hyper-focus on the sizable difference between Anne and the rest of us. It was as if we were the Shrinkies, though Anne looked nothing like Dr. Shrinker. She looked more like an enlarged version of another *Krofft Supershow* character, Electra Woman, which would logically make Mae her sidekick, Dyna Girl—my mind dressed them in skintight spandex. I noticed Chad observing Anne in the same manner, and he kept flashing me smiles I tried not to acknowledge. It was only a matter of time before he made a grossly inappropriate comment.

"Anne, I mean this question objectively, and not offensively, but what's larger?" Chad asked.

Here it comes.

"Your breast or your shotput?"

I scanned the nearest sheer wall to see if there were any handholds I could scramble up in case she Three Mile Island'd.

"Well, you should know," she said in the calmest of calms.

"But I've never held your shotput," Chad said, yesterday's amnesia cured.

"Good point," she said. "I guess I've never thought about it." With her right hand she cupped her right breast through her bikini, looked down, and bounced and turned it a bit. She paused while doing mental comparisons.

"A shotput is approximately four inches across, between twelve and thirteen inches around, and nine pounds," she said. "I would deduce my breast, though not perfectly round, at its widest point is slightly larger, but it weighs less."

"I appreciate the well-thought-out answer," replied Chad, as if this were a perfectly normal conversation. "And Anne?"

"Yes?"

"Please tell the truth. You've thought of that before."

After a few dead moments, "You're right."

We veered off into Phantom Canyon, a much narrower sheer-cliffed slot, and all of us instinctually looked to the sky before exiting our current drain into an even smaller one. There were a few random clouds now passing along the electric blue sky, but they were bright, white, and fluffy—the third-best-known American, Mr. Whipple, surely would have given them a squeeze. We encountered a few worn paths, likely animal trails, and we followed the most obvious one along the west side of Phantom Creek.

"Yes, we'll walk with a walk that is measured and slow," Mae said.

I replied from memory, "And we'll go where the chalk-white arrows go."

Anne added, "For the children, they mark, and the children, they know."

Even Chad knew this one, "The place where the sidewalk ends."

The grade of Phantom Canyon was much steeper, and the creek was an endless series of pools cascading over polished sandstone. We were treated to late spring color from clusters of magenta blooms on small western redbud trees speckling the landscape. We soon reached the two-tiered, twenty-five-foot waterfall, which was most noticeable for its eye-catching contrasts: bright green ferns grew in the grotto behind the white spray over the red rock. Unlike the water of the Colorado, tributary water was much clearer, and the pool at the bottom looked refreshing. Unfortunately, it was too shallow for swimming. Ponch said our destination was just beyond, so we scrambled up the rocks on the west side, past a few small feeder pools, before we reached a much larger holding tank. It was crystal clear, thirty-feet long, twenty-feet wide, deeper than a backyard pool, with a near-sheer wall on the east side. The morning shade split the pool laterally in half.

"Over there," Chad said, and pointed to a stair-like series of ledges on the wall, ascending about twenty-five feet.

"Right on," Anne said.

Chad left his stereo, with Steve Miller agonizing, *jungle love | it's drivin' me mad | it's makin' me crazy*, high up on a rock for better acoustics. He and Anne shed everything but their bathing suits, with the odd exception of his headband, at the water's edge.

"Cold!" Wolfman shrieked, as they swam to the natural stairs in the shade. Mae and I watched as Chad led Anne on a rapid ascent of the footholds; the extinguished six-pack masked any inhibitions or safety observations. At the pinnacle ledge, Chad jumped outward, easily clearing the wall, broke from shade into sun, landed cleanly in the middle of the pool, and let out a primitive scream when he surfaced.

"Far out," Anne said. "You didn't hit bottom?"

"Not even close."

"Here I come then. You better move."

"Go for it," Chad said, treading water. "I'll catch you," he jested, reaching his arms out.

Anne called his bluff and bounded off the wall. Chad only had time to duck under, and she landed on top of their totem pole. She surfaced, grimacing.

"Are you okay?" Mae asked.

"I'm going to have a head-sized bruise on my ass," Anne said.

Chad surfaced next to her, rubbing his neck.

"Why didn't you get out of the way, you dumb-ass," Anne said.

"How come no one felt sorry for the iceberg the *Titanic* hit?" Chad asked, smiling.

"You're so lame," Anne said, also smiling. These two *got* each other.

"Give it a try," Chad said to Mae and me. We stripped down to our suits and swam across. The water was cold, but not even close to San Diego winter surf. Mae followed me up the wall. The deep footholds and slant of the wall made it an easy path, though my steps became more tentative the higher we scaled. I imagined shoulder straps pulling me back again. Gravity sensed my fear and tried to take control. I leaned my whole body into the rock to distribute friction.

"Are you okay?" Mae asked.

"I'm fine. Why?"

"You're moving painfully slow, and you look like someone just said *stick 'em up.*"

"Sorry. I had a railing flashback. I'm having a little high anxiety."

"Don't psyche out."

"I won't."

We reached the top ledge, and I looked down while still facing the wall. It looked like it would be difficult to clear the lower part of the wall even though I had seen Chad and Anne do it easily. I turned my head and looked back at the ledges we climbed. I felt incapable of a descent. My heart raced and my palms began to sweat, which concerned me because I was gripping fissures as tightly as humanly possible.

"You going to jump backwards?" Mae asked. "Or, did you have a vision, Fiver, that something goes wrong here?"

"I just need to relax a little before facing out."

My best friend heartened me from below with, "Fucking jump, spaz."

Mae hummed a few notes from "Dueling Banjos," then asked, "Want to know why I kissed you?" Her unexpected question interrupted my train wreck of thought.

"Sure."

"I was curious what it'd be like."

"That's it?"

"Why else would you kiss someone?"

"Do you always satisfy your curiosity?" I asked.

"I learned recently you don't have an infinite amount of time to do all the things you want to do."

"And?" I asked.

"And what?"

"Did you enjoy it?"

"Sorry. I can't say unless you jump."

"That's square."

Her trick worked. I was completely at ease and turned my body outward. This was the perfect opportunity for me to shift to a more aggressive mental attitude, with the highly desired goal of Mae in mind.

Anne interrupted from below, "Let's make this more entertaining. Before you jump, you have to shout an overused phrase or quote you're tired of hearing. *Catch my drift?*"

I knew exactly what she was looking for. San Diego State was in the flight path of the airport, and not a day went by when some genius didn't exclaim, in diminutive Tattoo's French accent, *de plane, de plane.*

"Tastes great, less filling!" I shouted, stutter-stepped, then retreated my back against the wall.

"Remember," Mae said. "You don't have an infinite amount of time to do all the things you want to do. Jump on the count of five."

"Okay," I said, but my moist palms signaled I was losing the battle again.

Mae counted, "One, two…"

Although I was looking down at the sun reflecting off the water, I saw the oddest thing out of the corner of my eye—Mae's body was reflecting light.

"…three, four…"

As I turned to get a better look, she shoved me off the wall before reaching *five.* I broke out of the shadow into the sun, flailed my arms, and pierced the water, smiling the whole time while Mae yelled a long *yes!* When I surfaced, I looked up expecting to see the day's sun had found Mae's perch on the wall, but she was shaded and the illusion of light was gone.

Mae shouted into Phantom Canyon, "Who loves ya, baby?" and joined me in the pool.

A vicious climbing, shouting, launching, splashing cycle began.

Chad, "May the force be with you!" Jump.

Anne, "Kiss my grits!" Jump.

"Up your nose with a rubber hose!" I said, and jumped.

Mae, "Hey, don't knock masturbation. It's sex with someone I love!" Jump.

Chad, "You talkin' to me? You talkin' to me? You talkin' to me?" Cannonball.

Anne, "And remember, students, if you can't be an athlete, be an athletic supporter!" Cannonball. Nearly drained the pool.

"Was it over when the Germans bombed Pearl Harbor?" I exhorted, and jumped.

Mae called down that her brother loved that movie, before exclaiming, "Reach out and touch someone!" Cannonball.

Chad and I, with spasmodically jerking bodies, dangerous on a thin ledge, "We are...two wild and crazy guys!" Dual jump. Chad left the game on a creative high note and floated on his back. I climbed up again.

Anne and Mae, "Have a Coke and a smile," then "No Coke, Pepsi!" Dual jump.

Anne retired and joined Chad, showing him her shotputting technique with a rock, not breast, from shore. The current mix of awe and satisfaction in Chad's expression was one I had not witnessed before. It was obvious he was experiencing a new, original kind of feeling. Chad, and Suzy to an extent, had grown to rely on me to speak up as his voice of reason in situations where he faced temptation to stray. But as I surveyed the natural scenery, sounds, and smiles, it felt unnatural to intervene. While processing this, my mind distorted Chad's expression into one of inexplicable terror, and I had to shake my head to clear the random thought.

Mae did a television montage finale, "Nanu-nanu! Hey, *Hey, Hey!* Dyn-o-mite! What'chu talkin' 'bout, Willis? Marsha, Marsha, Marsha! G'night Johnboy!" Jump. She climbed the wall again to hang with me.

Although we had squeezed all of the creative juice out of this, I had something left to prove to the others, and myself. On the top ledge, I mentally processed the steps of a dive and readied my stance. Making sure I was heard above Steve Miller's "Jet Airliner" chorus, *oh, oh big ol' jet airliner | don't carry me too far away*, I yelled, "Yo, Adrian. I did it!"

Though I was mentally committed, a distant sound caused me to hesitate. It began as very quiet TV static and slowly grew. I scanned up and down the canyon looking for a rockslide, stampede, or any other source. Mae quickly scampered up the last few ledges to me to get a better view. It grew to a roar, and I looked to the sky for Steve Miller's Jet Airliner, or a low-flying helicopter tour, ready to do a trite Tattoo impression. The sky was empty. Anne, from the far shore, and Chad, treading water, looked up to Mae and me for answers. I noticed a change in the transparency of our swimming hole. The clear pool slowly clouded over mud brown from entry to exit. Mae and Anne noticed it too and, sensing something horrible, we all shouted at Chad to get out. The wall began vibrating, and Mae and I turned and flattened our bodies against it. My face was turned upstream, and I saw veins of reddish-brown water bank off the wall of a creek bend and race towards our pool. My eyes widened when I saw what gave chase and swallowed the veins. A five-foot-high wave of muddied water was raging through the Phantom drain. The noise became deafening, and tremors from boulder movement rocked our wall. I yelled *flood,* but whether anyone could hear me was doubtful.

I craned my neck and saw Anne's delayed reaction due to her lower angle. She took a few steps towards the pool, reached out a hand to Chad, but had to snap it back and run to higher ground. The wave crashed into and over the holding tank, and I witnessed the moment of impact when Chad, his face terror-stricken, was swallowed up. A vital part of me was violently ripped out. Chad's friendship, destined to be a lifelong one, had filled a companion-ship void left by my lack of siblings. My brother would imminently be crushed on the rocks after tumbling over the twenty-five-foot Phantom Creek Falls.

As the smell of wet clay filled my nostrils, I could not let go of the rock to turn and track his path. Mae was crying next to me, and Anne was trapped, safely, in an area of boulders between the west wall and the danger. She was scurrying around like a fenced-in dog trying to escape to her master. The flash flood was a dense, dark, reddish-brown mud with an arsenal of dangerous canyon de-bris: trees, cacti, dead animals, boulders, and, now, my best friend.

13. '01

Back in the room, we got ahold of Warren and sang an appall-ingly out-of-tune *Happy Birthday*. I felt the insecure need, to Mae's annoyance, to outsing her. Holding the receiver between us, we learned Warren was going to spend the day hiking Cold Spring Canyon with a girl from his dorms, and then go out to Rusty's Pizza with friends. I apologized for not being there, but he said he was kind of glad, wanting to spend as much time as possible with friends before coming home for the Christmas break. He men-tioned he needed advice on something, and when I told him *I'm all ears*, he asked if he could talk to just mom about it. I feigned indifference and wished him happy birthday again before relin-quishing the receiver.

Mae sat on the bed listening to and laughing with Warren while I paced the room. This was a frequent pattern I picked up on recently. Whether it was a conversation with Warren or his older sister, Hazel, at Pepperdine, I seemed to get the small talk, while Mae got the depth. Throughout their lives, I had always been there for them, ready to help whenever they needed it. And I had always offered proactive advice so they could make safe and prudent choices. When they sought Mae's help, her responses were usually *what do you think you should do* or *how would that make you feel?* It frustrated me because I did not understand why she would make a situation more complex, instead of solving it. She would watch them spin too fast and long on the merry-go-round, just so they understood consequences—regardless of the cleanup involved. On many occasions she even let them fail when it was clearly preventable. Would she let *us* fail?

I paced until the room got too small. When their conversation appeared to be open-ended, I wrote the word *Yavapai* on the hotel notepad, held it up until she acknowledged it with a nod, and left. Seeking validation, I tried calling Hazel from the lobby but got no answer. The thought of possibly having to tell my children that we were getting divorced was embarrassing, heartrending, and just plain wrong. And the thought of reverting back to only an observer of Mae—and possibly Mae plus a new lover—at the quintessential milestones in our kids' lives was devastating. The more my mind went down this path, the more dominoes fell. Exiting the El Tovar, I immediately felt a drop in temperature from earlier, and my hands sought my pockets. As I hurriedly walked the rim trail east towards Yavapai Point, it was obvious the fog was not dissipating, but thickening and darkening.

Propped right on the edge of the rim, the Yavapai Point Trailside Museum, built in 1928, blended seamlessly into its setting with indigenous Kaibab limestone rocks and ponderosa pine construction. I was hit by a wave of heat when I entered, and I instinctively shook both arms and let out a grunt. Two rangers, the only people in there, looked up, annoyed, from their desk and an *Electronic Battleship* game. The blond and dark-haired Hispanic looked familiar. The gears in my mind tried to find a match.

There were two sections to the museum: a gift shop, and a science area focusing on the geologic story of the canyon. A whole wall of windows provided unobstructed views into the canyon—if it was still there. Conscious of being the only customer, I busied myself at an interactive exhibit where you could pick up rock samples from each of the canyon's layers. The door to the museum opened and I anxiously looked to see if it was Mae. I should have yearned for our discussion to begin, yet, when someone else entered, I breathed a sigh of relief. It was an attractive female, surprisingly all by herself, and the Hispanic ranger bounded up to offer her a tour. His assertive behavior prompted my recollection of these same two rangers checking us into Phantom Ranch twenty-two years ago. They wouldn't recall me, but I couldn't forget their resemblance to *CHiPs* Officers Baker and Poncherello.

Perhaps Mae was prioritizing other activities over our discussion, maybe even reconsidering whether it was necessary at all. Conceivably, in my opinion at least, the current state of our marriage was something we could make minor fixes to, tune-ups, instead of deconstructing the whole thing. It was a pure bullshit thought. Though I was better than she was at ignoring issues, I knew our original connection, foundation, and deepest layer had incurred severe damage, putting everything above it at risk.

As I fondled a 500-million-year-old pale green piece of Bright Angel shale, I observed a quote written in large font above the view windows: *Given enough time, nothing is more changeable than rock.* The erosion of the Grand Canyon took five million to six million years. Ours took only twenty-two. The canyon's bottom layer was two billion years old. Ours was only three days.

Although our relationship was a whole, created and defined by the integration of Mae's half with mine, I carried the burden of knowing I fell the farthest from the person I promised I would be. I couldn't pinpoint the first seemingly inconsequential self-serving choice I made since Mae and I met, but I knew each one chipped away at her trust and respect, and our foundation; they fed off each other, and there had been a multitude. My choices had devolved from altruistic to always, first and foremost, considering how they impacted me. It was an easy slope to slide down, especially the more I got away with it. I had created this opportune universe centered on me, and it felt...monumentally empty. Snowflakes pattered the windows, infrequent and insignificant at first. They morphed into a furious onslaught, their strength in numbers weighing me down, and I struggled mightily not to cry in front of Baker and Ponch.

14. '79

Mae spotted something downstream and screamed like a banshee. I had to push off a little from the wall to look around her, which I cautiously did while my fingertips kept a Peter Parker–tight grip. Where the holding tank had previously calmly cascaded into a lower, smaller pool, the elevation change and segue were now seamless, aside from a few smaller stalled boulders. About four feet directly downstream from those boulders, an arm—Chad's arm—had a death-grip on a drooping magenta branch of a western redbud growing out of a large fissure between the side rocks. Where there should have been a transition from his bicep to shoulder, neck, and head, it was bicep to mud. The rest of his body was submerged. My eyes immediately picked up on an incorrect law of physics: his arm was pointing downstream, not upstream, so somehow he was pinned backwards in the flood.

The forearm and bicep muscles of the bodiless arm tightened, and a slimy reddish-brown forehead, nose, and pair of lips momentarily broke the surface, then disappeared again. Mae noticed it too, and we were both scanning our wall to see if there was any available path in his direction. Our previous footholds disappeared into the raised floodwater, and based on the bighorn sheep carcass floating below us, crossing was not an option.

Mae and I both did what any commoners would do in a situation like this—we yelled for a superhero, "Anne!"

Anne could not see downstream due to where she was trapped in the rocks, but she could see us pointing and knew she was being called to action. I kept my eyes on her, curious how she would handle her transformation. Unlike *Wonder Woman*'s alter ego, Diana Prince, she did not spin, and there was no bright flash of light like on *Electra Woman and Dyna Girl*. She took Jaime Sommers's casual *Bionic Woman* approach, which required no costume change, and made a series of grabs, hoists, stretches, and leaps through an ominously thick blockade of rocks, to reach a spot on shore about seven feet upstream of Chad's arm. My mind had accompanied the acrobatics with the required bionic sound effect: *dun-nuh-nuh-nuh-nuh.*

There was too dangerous of a gap between her current position and Chad's arm, so she tentatively, leaning back in a semi-squat, entered the flood north of the gathered boulders. The sludge was up to her knees as she baby-stepped to the rock pile and leaned forward to use it as a brace. She slowly lowered her squat, keeping herself stable with her right hand on a rock, and plunged her left arm below the surface. It was submerged beyond her shoulder as she felt around the rocks for Chad's body. My eyes stayed affixed on where I last saw his face, and I couldn't tell if I saw it resurface again or if my mind projected a prayerful replay. I contemplated how, in addition to the grieving, I would be psychologically fucked-up if I was witnessing his slow, torturous death. There was a heavy cost attached to the new hope Anne provided. Our wall was still shaking from debris contact, a reminder that at any moment another boulder could pin Anne in a crushing sandwich. After a half-minute of dredging, she pulled her mud-caked arm out of the flood, turned towards us, and pointed at one of the rocks.

Most of the rock was submerged, with the reddish-brown flow surfing over it, making it hard to judge its size. Anne positioned herself closely behind it, crouched down in an extreme squat where her entire midsection went under, and plunged both arms below the surface and around the rock. My mind sounded *dun-nuh-nuh-nuh-nuh* to help. Her legs straightened, but her back remained bent and arms sunken, as her first attempt at a lift failed. She bent her knees again and this time let out a guttural scream sure to be heard across all 1,904 square miles of the park. This must have been her method of transformation, because she threw her head back and used every ounce of every muscle fiber in her body—and ten additional bodies—and the rock began to rise. Even from my distance I could see the veins fighting to escape her body.

Holding the branch with his hand, which turned out to be his left, Chad's body dragged downstream. I could not breathe, waiting for either the fatigued arm or roots to give out. In this new precarious position, facing and swallowing the mudflow, he had to use some of Anne's leftover superhuman strength to reach past his head with his right hand and grab the branch. His mud-caked frame slowly pulled itself up and out, hand over hand, until he was able to secure a higher-up hold on the rock, enough to clear the sludge flow. Mae's tears of dread turned to contagious ones of joy. I felt my body slowly refill with past and future memories the flood had attempted to steal away.

Chad, hoarsely coughing to clear his lungs, was coated reddish-brown from head to toe and was chameleon-like against the rock. Remarkably, his headband was still in place. His bathing suit must have been wedged up his butt because the slot was clearly visible, even through his new outer skin. I could not help but release an inappropriate laugh. Mae, spotting the same crack in the mud, joined me.

After Anne tossed aside—yes—tossed aside, not dropped—no—not dropped, the meteor, and the flow subsided a little, she was able to scale the rock over to Chad and piggyback him back to the safe shore. He dismounted, got down on his hands and knees, and began violently throwing up mud. It was an unpleasant, disturbing sight—very wrong end. Anne supported him from the side in case he passed out. A few minutes later, after the flood receded enough, Mae and I climbed down and breaststroked across the thinning muck with our lips tightly sealed. Chad remained on all fours, taking deep breaths into his dirtied lungs. From the side, camouflaged in mud, Chad looked primal. At first I thought it was the filth, but after more scrutiny I realized it was because he was buck naked under that slop, with the exception of his goofy headband.

Out of respect for his discomfort, Mae and Anne covered their mouths to hold laughter hostage. I tried and failed; he was too *National Geographic.* Complicating matters, our shirts, shorts, sandals, hats, and daypack had been way too close to the creek and were likely sailing by Phantom Ranch at this point. We would all be barefooting it back in only our bathing suits, except for Chad, who had one layer less.

The Aborigine sluggishly rose and cupped his crotch with his hands. With a look of awe, he thanked Anne profusely, spraying her with mud spittle in the process. Mae and I also profoundly praised her for saving his life. Blushing from the spotlight, Anne now sported organic reddish-brown knee-high tube socks and long sleeves, and mud-caked bikini bottoms. I reminded Chad he wanted a memorable weekend and he grinned, reflecting on the near tragedy.

Surprisingly, he felt okay, aside from a strong need for a toothbrush and mouthwash, and asked the girls if either would walk back topless so he could rig a penis hammock out of a bikini top. Both politely declined. With no other options, he casually removed the muddy headband and stepped his right leg through it. He pulled it all the way up so it flossed between his butt cheeks, and then used the front of the loop to split his nuts and try to hold his penis back in a sling. He did it casually, as if this were one of its intended uses. Linus would have gotten more coverage from his blanket. We were in hysterics watching him try to line things up perfectly. There was no *perfectly*; a little bit always spilled out.

Like a faithful pet, Chad's stereo was waiting for us on higher ground where it had been left, tamely quiet after reaching the end of side two. Hiking back, it was hard for me to decide which was more uncomfortable, walking in front of, or behind, Chad—an unsettling visual either way. Ultimately, we made it a point to walk side-by-side with him, resembling a gang, much less intimidating than the Riffs, Rogues, Punks, or Baseball Furies from *The Warriors*; perhaps the Canyonites, or ABBA after a really bad day.

As we approached Phantom Ranch, Anne took off running ahead. I assumed she was seeking a ranger to report our safe return, but instead, when she shouted, "Early man! Early man! We've found Neanderthal man in the Grand Canyon!" I realized she just wanted to make an ass out of Chad. The ranch guests goggled and laughed at the creature we brought back. Chad took off sprinting towards our cabin with a big smile on his face. As he galloped— four cheeks blushing—it was scientifically proven the mudsling was unable to structurally hold up under increased speed.

15. '79

I could not remember Chad ever smiling this large with Suzy. He appreciated Anne's brashness, but I knew he also appreciated Suzy, though she was completely the opposite. While my parents drifted apart, I noticed they stopped acknowledging each other's strengths and gifts. How could they have become so blind to qualities so glaring and obvious when they met? Or, had those qualities faded from a lack of appreciation?

While mudsling and his heroine opted to take a nap for the second afternoon in a row, Mae and I got sack lunches at the canteen and ate outside. We again watched Ranger Carroll on his continuous loop around the ranch, always pausing at the field in front of the employee bunkhouse, and never too distant from his wife. Baker and Ponch came over to say hello. Ponch proposed Mae round up some of the other female guests, have them throw on bathing suits, and he would referee a game of volleyball. Baker, embarrassed by Ponch's counsel, suggested Mae and I walk to the Colorado to watch rafts shoot the rapids. I would have been fine with either, but I let Mae decide.

The two of us hiked to the Silver Suspension Bridge, but instead of crossing the Colorado, we turned downstream along the shore. Though not a mapped trail, there was an obvious path through the sand and rocks. Mae led the way on the single track. She had added a replacement pair of cutoffs to her avocado green bikini. I had added a replacement tee, black with the name of a San Diego punk band, the Cardiac Kidz, to my bathing suit. Our sandals, also victims of the morning flood, were replaced by hiking boots. I carried a canteen for us.

"People recently in the news," Mae said.

"What?" I asked.

"The category is people in the news. Start with the first initial of the previously said last name. Got it?"

"I'm a college graduate. I know how to play the name game. I've just never tried it sober."

"I'll start," she said. "Keith Moon."

"Moon the Loon," I said. Keith, the drummer for the Who, died last year from an overdose. "He ran over his chauffeur and blew up hotel toilets. Are you a Who fan?"

"I am," she said. "You?"

"Absolutely. Favorite song?"

"'My Generation.' Yours?"

"'Who Are You.'"

"Keith was a mess, but an incredible musician," she said. "Did you know what his last words were, the night he overdosed?"

"No."

"If you don't like it, you can fuck off!"

"That's a great last line. My turn. Magic Johnson."

"Who?" she asked.

"He was the star of the college basketball team that won the national championship this year."

"Athlete. Figures. Is his name really Magic?"

"Nickname. It's Earvin."

"Then you lost the game already."

"Give me a break. Would you want to be called Earvin? Mark my words, he'll be famous someday."

"Yeah, I'm sure he'll bring a lot of attention to important social issues with his ability to score," she said sarcastically.

As Mae contemplated her *J* options, I eyed the river for potential heat relief. Ranger Baker had explicitly said swimming was a death wish because of the flow force and temperature. The river was currently flowing at about 25,000 cubic feet per second, and he said to think of a cubic foot as a basketball. In one second, all those basketballs rolled through a given point—an intimidating visual. And the water was only forty-six degrees. I wore a full wetsuit surfing if the San Diego ocean temperature dropped below sixty-eight degrees.

"Jim Jones," she said.

"This is a cheerful game," I said. "That gave me nightmares." Jim Jones led a U.S. church, the People's Temple, whose members committed a mass suicide last year in a remote compound, Jonestown, in South America.

"Incredibly sad," she said. "You know why he moved his church from San Francisco to South America?"

"I can't remember. Why?"

"An article was about to come out about him physically, mentally, and sexually abusing church members."

"So he escaped?" I said.

"Basically. And when a congressman went and investigated the compound, he discovered some members were being held hostage, so Jones's followers shot him. Jones knew this meant the end of his church and convinced—or forced—912 of his followers, including 276 children, to drink grape flavoring mixed with cyanide and Valium."

As my mind indexed for a more uplifting *J*, I paid more attention to her cutoffs than where I was stepping, often tripping on the jagged rocks. She kept glancing across the river at the afternoon River trail hikers, and then would turn her head one degree further to steal a quick glimpse of me. I could feel the physical pull growing between us.

"John Wayne," I said.

"I knew you'd say him."

"How?"

"You wanted to lighten things up from Jim Jones, so you decided to pick a celebrity. John Ritter probably came to mind first because you're a Jack Tripper fan, but you didn't want to appear too shallow. Then after your mind stalled on an image of Suzanne Somers, you considered John Denver, but didn't want to appear too sensitive. Then John Travolta, but no guy would ever admit he liked *Grease*, even though every one of you did. And after your mind stalled again, this time on Olivia Newton-John, you decided to go with the man's man to appear strong."

"I went with him because the guy died this week," I said. "I'm paying my respects to a movie legend. Plus, you seemed to prefer dead names." I lied; my mind worked exactly how she assumed.

"Were you a fan?" she asked.

"Tomorrow is the most important thing in life," I said. "Comes into us at midnight very clean. It's perfect when it arrives and it puts itself in our hands. It hopes we've learned something from yesterday."

Mae stopped and stared at me. "That's beautiful. Did John Wayne say that?"

"Yes. I read it in *Playboy*."

"Figures."

We passed the point on the other side of the river where the Bright Angel trail began.

"William Shatner," she said.

"An actor? Isn't that too obvious for you?" I asked.

"I'm a huge *Star Trek* fan. Sci-fi overall."

I stopped hiking. Even with the roar of the river, she noticed the cessation of my footsteps and stopped and looked back at me.

"What?" she asked.

"I've made that statement many times and people usually think I'm square," I said. "It's refreshing to hear someone else say it out loud. You know the movie is coming out later this year."

"I know," she said. "The new TV series, *Star Trek: Phase II*, was supposed to come out last year, but it got replaced by the movie after the success of *Star Wars* and *Close Encounters of the Third Kind*."

"Do you think it will be any good?" I asked.

"Bigger than *Star Wars*," she said.

"*Star Wars* was the highest grossing movie ever. They're making two sequels."

"Bigger!"

"Do you think they're really cancelling *Battlestar Galactica* after only one season?" I asked.

"No way. ABC is trying to create more interest by teasing us."

"Have you seen *Alien*?"

"First day. Scared the crap out of me. Loved it. You?"

"Freaked me out, too. What did you think of *Superman*?"

"Silly and shouldn't have been made," she said. "What will they try to reinvent and ruin next, *Batman*?"

"Suzanne Somers," I said, returning us to the game from our sci-fi tangent.

"Predictable. I shouldn't have mentioned her name. You have the poster of her wearing a blue bathing suit?" she asked.

"Guilty."

"What other posters do you have that debase women?"

"Cheryl Tiegs, Lynda Carter, Susan Anton, Farrah Fawcett, and...the receptionist from WKRP?...Loni Anderson. Which ones do you have?"

"I outgrew poster porn a few years ago. I had the basics: both *Hardy Boys*, Leif Garrett, and Andy Gibb."

"What about that guy from *Battlestar Galactica*?" I asked.

"Dirk Benedict? I'd take a starfuck from Lieutenant Starbuck."

I smiled but was not sure how to react to her crudeness. Rarely did I hear the *f* word used as a verb by a female.

Our makeshift path ended and we were forced to scamper over rocks, while occasionally walking through the river's shallow edge. I was amazed how cold the water felt compared to Phantom Creek.

"Sid Vicious," she said.

"Were you a Sex Pistols fan?" I asked. Sid Vicious, the Sex Pistols bassist, died recently from an overdose. Last year he was accused of killing his girlfriend Nancy in a drugged stupor.

"I loved them. You?"

"Not at first, but after their album got played at every single party, they grew on me. Favorite song?

"'Anarchy in the U.K.,'" she said. "You?"

"'Holidays in the Sun.'"

"Do you use drugs?" Mae asked.

"I've tried a lot of stuff, but I only smoke a little weed. You?"

"I'm clean. I think life needs to be dealt with naturally. And, grass makes me paranoid."

We ran out of land and were forced to wade knee deep as we leaned into the rock wall. Our game, which continued to usually be her tragic figures balanced by my pop culture, petered out as our footing became more precarious. The shore widened again right before the Horn Creek rapid location Baker described. A large rock pier jutted into the river in the middle of the steep rapid and we took a seat. The loud, turbulent water sounded like an airliner taking off and I commented on it. Continuing her penchant for sad tales, Mae mentioned the crash of American Airlines flight 191 in Chicago a few weeks earlier, the deadliest ever on U.S. soil.

"I don't know why the Colorado's so damn cold when it's like a sauna down here," I commented.

"It's our fault it's so *dam* cold," Mae said.

"What do you mean?"

"Because we *dammed* it."

"Meaning?"

"The Glen Canyon Dam was built upstream of the Grand Canyon to regulate the flow and generate power. That's how Lake Powell formed. The canyon water now comes from well below the lake surface, and the temperature and flow no longer have extreme seasonal swings."

"Consistent is nice," I said.

"No, it's not," she said. "Without the seasonal changes, native fish aren't prompted to spawn and their populations are dwindling, and the lack of natural flooding is causing an overgrowth of vegetation. This Colorado bears little in common with the old one. It used to carry large amounts of sand and soil, which is why it was named *Colorado*, Spanish for red. Now the dam traps the sediment, and the water is clear. The sandbars and islands need sediment and are eroding away."

Two black and gold rafts floated into view a few hundred yards upstream. Each carried six paddlers and a guide. One hundred yards out, the paddles entered the water and synchronized a few well-executed strokes, propelling the boats towards a small beach on our side of the river. The two guides jumped out, anchored the boats to shore, and hiked down to our rock to scout the rapid. They were the spitting images of Delta Tau Chi pledges Lawrence *Pinto* Kroger and Kent *Flounder* Dorfman from *Animal House*. I opted to keep my doppelgänger comment to myself after the Baker and Ponch episode. They gave us an infectiously happy greeting—the kind you get from individuals who do not view their job as work. They first scouted Mae's bikini top, then the water's path and movements.

Mae decided to get their *dam* opinion, "Guys, is the dam good or bad for rafting?"

"Both," the skinny, dopey-grinned Pinto said. "Good because we can raft year round. Bad because without floods the river is unable to carry away rockslides, creating more dangerous rapids. And, more drownings occur because of hypothermia from the colder water."

I irritably noticed Pinto was scouting Mae's bikini top again.

"Gotta 8-track player on board," he continued. "Do you have any tune requests for when we shoot the rapid? Just bought the Knack."

"Got any Sex Pistols?" Mae asked.

"Yeah, baby!" Pinto exclaimed.

"'Anarchy in the U.K.'?"

"Outta sight."

The heavyset Flounder looked pissed at Pinto for propositioning Mae first. Awkwardly, he asked me, "What about you; any requests? Something besides 'My Sharona,' which my square buddy has played twenty times on this trip?"

"Got any Who?" I asked.

"Dude, I never float without them," Flounder said.

"'Who Are You'?"

"Right on."

Mae stood up and reached her hand out to Pinto and Flounder, "Hi, Mae, Grand Canyon tourist, damn glad to meet you." Apparently, she noticed the *Animal House* resemblance also.

I stood up and extended my hand, "Hi, that was Mae, Grand Canyon tourist. She was damn glad to meet you."

Their wan smiles disclosed they were not virgins to this greeting. As Pinto and Flounder hiked back to their boats, Mae sported a quizzical expression, which had me scanning above her head for a light bulb.

"What?" I asked.

"I feel like singing out loud with their tunes."

"Okay," I said. She could have just done it. Not sure why she shared in advance.

"It would be more fun if you did it, too," she said.

"Would love to," I said. "But I don't know the words to 'Anarchy in the U.K.'"

"You know the words to 'Who Are You,' though, right?"

I should lie. I should lie. I should lie. "I suppose."

"Then we can each do our own song."

"Do I have any choice in the matter?"

"You always have a choice. It's what you do with those choices that defines you."

I could tell any shot with Mae was over if I was not willing to do something outside my comfort zone. "Cool beans."

Pinto's boat launched off the beach first. As promised, an 8-track player, presumably located somewhere dry, started blasting "Anarchy in the U.K." Even with the rumble of the rapids, the guitar intro cleanly filled the canyon's void. Our rock pier became Mae's stage and she stood at the very end facing her audience— me. As the raft picked up speed near the mouth of the rapids, her whole body tensed as she sang with Johnny Rotten into her pretend microphone/right hand, *I am an anti-Christ | I am an anarchist | don't know what I want | but I know how to get it | I wanna destroy passerby | 'cause I wanna be anarchy.*

Anger invaded her voice, though it was not that of the disenfranchised British youth the song represented. Her anger originated from someplace else—someplace real—and her face looked out of control and ready to slip into laughter or sorrow at any moment. Although I would normally be scanning every inch of a beautiful female singer's body while watching her on stage, her eyes were locked on mine and I could tell she sought trust and support, not someone to look at her as an object.

As the raft shot between two big boulders, the *horns*, at the top of the Horn Creek rapid, Mae, ignorant of the action behind her, jumped into the second verse and...*it* happened again—she illuminated. This time there was definitely no assistance from the sun. The radiation came from inside and traced the outline of her figure. It was the type of fluorescent shape found within the darkness of eyelids. I looked to see if any of the rafters noticed, but with paddles in their laps while they leaned towards the center of the craft, they were more focused on not flipping.

As Pinto steered the miniscule amount the tumultuous chute of whitewater allowed, and the miraculously dry 8-track player continued, Mae sang on. She was powerful, passionate, and alive as possible up there. With the uninterrupted eye contact, I felt something more internal than external taking place. She was intimately opening up, risking extreme vulnerability by baring her soul through song. And she chose me for this. Sure, my only competitors were pledges Pinto and Flounder, but I was a recent college graduate, and they had three more years at Faber—assuming they could raise their respective grade point averages from 1.2 and .2, and successfully appeal their expulsions.

With a guitar break between lyrics, Mae turned and faced the river. Right in front of our perch, 25,000 basketballs pushed Pinto's raft off course and over a boulder that had only a few inches of water capping it. Like at the peak of a roller coaster, the raft slowed with the friction. Screams erupted as it pitched steeply over the lip and folded up like a taco in the water. When the taco shell opened, the ingredients released a collective roar. Caught in an eddy, the raft's forward momentum ceased and it was pulled back towards the boulder. Under the lip, the basketballs cascaded off Pinto's helmet, and he ordered a hard forward paddle. The rafters dug deep to break out of the boulder's tractor beam (I could not remember whether I first saw this effect in *Star Trek* or *Star Wars*). The moment Mae entered her third verse, they broke free and continued their journey into the mellower second half of the rapid.

We both cheered, and to make the moment unforgettable, Mae flipped up her bikini top and gave the crew a quick peep. Pinto almost fell off the stern. I swore I saw his devil-outfitted evil conscience pop up on his shoulder. My conscience was divided on whether to be turned on, or concerned, by Mae's free spirit. With Pinto's raft downriver, the tunes were not as audible as Mae delivered her last line, *'cause I wanna be anarchy | it's the only way to be.* Below the rapid, Pinto and his passengers stood up, turned towards us, and clapped. As Mae took a bow, her glow faded.

We heard the instantly recognizable synthesizer and bass intro to "Who Are You," and turned upstream to see Flounder's raft had launched. I could still back out; I had many times in my life when things got uncomfortable, and regret got easier with practice. Yet, I knew unreserved girls like this did not give conservative guys like me second chances. Before I had a chance to change my mind, Mae went over and sat in the identical spot I had sat as her audience. She looked considerably more excited for this than I was. Two horny young adults singing British rock songs next to a violent rapid in the Grand Canyon—so cliché.

The lyrics began with a chorus of backup vocals. I sang along, *who are you? | who, who, who, who?* Mae sang along also, confusing me. She motioned that she would handle the backup vocals. Flounder angled his crew towards the far side of the rapid. Perfect! Less chance they would hear me as I joined Roger Daltrey, *I woke up in a Soho doorway | a policeman knew my name | he said 'you can go sleep at home tonight | if you can get up and walk away.'* Because of the competing white noise of the river, I could not hear how off-key I sounded, but my volume was high, and my eyes never left my audience of one. So far, it did not appear she wanted her money back. I cupped my ears in an attempt to block out the river, and as I delivered the second verse I realized I looked like I was pretending to be in a recording studio. If I was going to look stupid, I might as well abuse it.

Flounder entered the rapid just inside the far-side horn. Like its predecessor, Flounder's raft was in the river's control and he was only there for damage control. I took off my studio headphones and yelled, *well, who are you?*

Mae stood up and deflected my inquiry with her sole line, *who are you? | who, who, who, who?*

I stepped towards her, increased my volume, and reemphasized, *I really wanna know.*

We volleyed back and forth, never breaking eye contact, with ascending volume, intensity, and closeness. This was better than sex. After our confrontation, I turned from her and, because it felt right, strutted back towards the river. Flounder's crew approached the shallow boulder and eddy, but because of their altered path, it was not in their way.

I ripped into the next few verses at a decibel the fish could hear. My head was swollen from my newfound celebrity, and for a moment I forgot where Mae was. Downriver from us, Flounder's raft hit a berm and a female passenger tumbled out sideways. The river swallowed her. Flounder did not act concerned. The helmeted passenger popped up like a cork about five yards downstream of her entry. Her life preserver kept her well afloat as she bobbed on her back with feet forward, ready to kick off anything in her way.

I faced Mae and redemanded, *well, who are you?*

Mae held her ground, *who are you? | who, who, who, who?*

I really wanna know, I yelled and neared her again.

Mae did the same with her question.

I advanced and gazed deep inside of her as I delivered Daltrey's obscenity, *who the fuck are you?* I truly wanted to know.

The Who's volume dropped as Flounder sailed downstream. Pinto's raft, which had been waiting below the rapid, readied to scoop up the swimmer.

Mae countered at a lower volume and moved closer. Our faces were mere inches apart and she closed her eyes.

I really wanna know, I matched her volume and leaned in.

Who are you? | who, who, who, who?, she whispered, so close I felt her warm breath on my lips.

Clapping from Flounder's downstream boat interrupted our courting interrogation. I bowed to them and smiled at Mae.

"How do you feel?" Mae asked.

"Alive." For the first time ever, I felt *more than* capable in life. What else could I accomplish that I never considered before?

"Thank you," she said. "That's the first time in a while I've been able to *not* think, which is a good thing."

"Do you do stuff like that a lot?" I asked.

"My brother was a handful for my parents and he got most of their attention. When our family played hide-and-seek, no one looked for me. I learned to do just about everything at a high volume. We should head back before Chad and Anne worry."

My mind was in overdrive, wondering if someone like Mae could be a catalyst, an enabler, an inspiration, for me to accomplish greater things in life. How could the dormant pieces of my personality become active unless I was with someone possessing the correct ignition key? Hidden strengths were wasted if not uncovered. Could she make my life story more interesting?

More importantly, though, what could I do for her story? What impact would my character have? Would I create page-turning anticipation and excitement, or pedestrian subject matter and predictability? How could I convert a chance meeting over a few days into something by design and long term? And why was it important for her to *not* think? I was thinking the whole time during our performances—thinking how freeing it felt, and how opportunistic the future was finally looking.

Mae was silent as we walked. Her mind had retreated someplace. I respected wherever she was and thought deeply on what my next move would be. For a few brief seconds, it sounded like the Colorado amplified its roar, and when I glanced over, my out-of-water body could inexplicably feel the mighty tow of the torrential current, and I instinctively closed my mouth to avoid swallowing water that I wasn't even submerged in. Mae strolled on, indifferent to my momentary lapse, passing the small beach Pinto and Flounder had parked on. She spotted something, walked over, and picked up the yellow sleeve of the Sex Pistols' *Never Mind the Bollocks* 8-track. She sat down, removed her boots and socks, buried her feet in the sand, clasped her hands in front of propped-up knees, and stared blankly at the Colorado. Was this a move, Potsie? I sat next to her and set our empty canteen down.

A dead cottonwood leaf spiraled from the sky at a forty-five-degree angle, executed a perfect floatplane landing in front of us, and drifted downstream. Mae tracked its progress with more interest than it deserved, and her eyes widened as the suction of the rapids sped the defenseless leaf up. When it disappeared into the rush of whitewater, her eyes closed and her mouth clenched. She drew in a deep breath, opened her eyes and stared at me. Random strands of hair thinly veiled her face. Instinctually, I reached over and tucked them behind her ear. She did not flinch or respond. Though she was looking at me, her focus was inward.

Then I saw it, too. I knew. *The Drifters, Love Story, Ordinary People, What Dreams May Come*, Keith Moon, Sid Vicious, Jonestown, flight 191—tragedies, young deaths, survivor's guilt. She wanted to *not* think of *something*. My eyes glazed over as I held her stare.

"How long ago did it happen?" I asked.

"Two months."

"Who?"

"My twin brother."

"What happened?"

"Suicide."

16. '01

After waiting for Mae at Yavapai Point for an hour, as everything outdoors was painted white, I gave up and returned to the El Tovar. I found her comfortably alone in our room, having assumed I would have returned shortly after it started snowing. She had transitioned from counseling our son to counseling her best friend, Anne, whom she was on the phone with when I entered. I only heard small talk, and when I inquired about the substance of the discussion after she hung up, *girl talk* was apparently a comprehensive enough answer. Her eyes were puffy and red again.

The trinity of bad weather, inactivity, and boredom steered us back to the dining room. It was crowded with others lacking anything else to do, but we landed a premium table by the view windows. Beyond the snow, melting on the warmed glass and blanketing the outside deck and nearby landscape, it was still a gray void. An instrumental version of a serendipitous song from our past provided background music. Mae smiled from her recognition of the Australian duo we met in the canyon.

Another face-to-face sit down meal; another perfect opportunity to begin *the* discussion. When the waiter took our orders, I threw an inside reference/diversion at Mae, *wanna get drunk?*

She dimpled. "Why not."

A Miller Lite and house chardonnay accompanied our Navajo tacos. It was a minor victory; an optimistic activity we could do together; one that stimulated her passions and got her excited about life's possibilities, while ignoring dire consequences.

We were both fervent readers and I initiated a discussion about our recent yarns. I used to read anything I got my hands on, but now gravitated towards spy novels and thrillers, fast page-turners providing diversions with low-effort thought—not the best fodder for spousal conversations. In our early years we would read many of the same books, including a lot of philosophical, character-driven, and science fiction, and share our opinions. This often led to passionate, heated arguments which she enjoyed—but I didn't. I had learned to avoid them.

A couple glasses of wine triggered her telling a detailed version of the pinnacle cringe-worthy scene in *Garp* involving adultery, castration, and a child's death. The deep analyzation of dark themes, and strong female characters, were a staple of her literary choices. She always wanted to know what broke people, and what healed them. Symptoms were too material; she wanted root causes. After we paid the bill, Mae fished in her purse for her Freshen-up gum. When she produced a key instead and held it up in amazement, it took me a second to register the significance.

"Please tell me that's not the Barretts' house key," I said.

She nodded.

"What time are their moving trucks arriving Monday?" I asked.

"Noon."

"We can't get back that quickly." We were driving back Monday, but it was an eight-hour haul.

"You've got to overnight it to them," she said.

"Let's go do it together."

"I want to call them immediately to explain, and you haven't got a second to spare with the post office."

"Okay, but meet me in the lounge after," I said.

"All right."

Three Miller Lites, black ice, shallow Cutlass treads, and little experience driving in inclement weather made the few minute excursion to the South Rim Post Office a hairy one. Pathetically, I would have welcomed a single-vehicle car crash, with recoverable injuries, of course, if it would generate short-term compassion and a diversion. It saddened and scared me that I was even able to produce this thought.

The lone postal worker behind the counter, a kind elderly lady, assured me a late afternoon delivery would be made to Williams and a Monday morning San Diego arrival was guaranteed. John Denver tunes kept hitting the flippers in my head as I stared out the front windows of the post office into the wooded scenery and endless hypnotic snowfall. It had not let up since this morning, and if my digital Timex had not told me otherwise, I would have thought time was frozen. Two posters flanked my view, one for a *Star Wars* sequel they were showing a special presentation of at the visitor center—I could not believe they were *still* making sequels— and one for a Creedence Clearwater Revival reunion tour stop in Flagstaff—about time they got back together.

While my eyes blurred out endless rows of flurries, they brought into focus two people outside. Even in a snowstorm, in their inadequate summer uniforms of long pants, short sleeves, and hats, the young park rangers looked eternally happy. Their posture was perfect in their classic ballroom dancing pose: His right hand was behind her back and his left hand held her right hand at shoulder-level. Her left hand rested on his shoulder. Both faces were animated, their eyes angled into each other's, and her lips were slightly parted, as if she were singing to him in an old-fashioned musical. They had to know they were being watched, dancing on top of a picnic table directly in front of the post office. It stirred up a memory from my first few days with Mae.

The postal worker was also watching them. Her warm smile revealed she could see, and feel, the love between these two, as if it were personal. Doris Day sang, *gonna take a sentimental journey | gonna set my heart at ease | gonna make a sentimental journey | to renew old memories,* out of the overhead speakers attached to the exposed rafters of the nearly seventy-year-old rustic timber and stone structure. I was hesitant to leave the relaxed, heated room, armed with only my cotton sweatshirt to fight the elements—elements not bothering the two dancing rangers in the least.

Mae and I worked together, like the ranger couple; only I could not remember any on-the-clock dancing or prolonged animated eye contact. Neither one of us planned on long-term careers in real estate, especially Mae, but it was the trail life took us on, and it provided a comfortable lifestyle for our family. We worked for ourselves, which Mae appreciated, but the day-to-day activities were routine and predictable, which she deplored. There was always room for growth, adding sales or employees, but it was more of the same and not the change that Mae desired. At her insistence on many, many occasions, we had discussed making career switches; each time I convinced her to stay the conservative course. The only vocational area we were in complete agreement on was how our self-employment had satisfied our mutual desire for excess and impromptu vacations, where the escapism masked over most of our differences.

Outside of the post office, I brushed the snow off the placard on the bronzed picnic table with the two dancing statues on top. *Commemorating 75 years of dedicated service by the Grand Canyon National Park Rangers—These two happened to fall in love on the job.*

17. '79

What could I say? Growing up an only child, I never shared a bubble bath, was a tattletale or a victim of one, got to respond *hit* when a sibling said *B2*, fought over who rode in the front seat or got the last cookie, waited for a bathroom, or entrusted a secret to someone under the same roof. Independence and isolation had been my reality. Mae grew up relating daily to someone who was as integral to her life as air, water, and sleep, and then had that person instantly and permanently removed from her existence without warning, by his own hand, generating not only loss and a void, but collateral damage of guilt, second guesses, and unanswerable questions. This was so foreign to my mind and heart that neither knew how to begin processing it. Were there even words for this? I wanted to ask the *how* and *why*, but those were for my own curiosity, which was manifestly unimportant here. I confessed, "I don't know what to say."

"No one does. You can't solve it with words. I feel like I'm in my own universe, with extra gravity, like I'm always wearing my backpack even when it's off."

"Interesting," I said. "I'm not comparing the two situations, but ever since the railing yesterday, I've felt like my pack is permanently attached and could pull me backwards and out of control at any moment."

She gave me a quizzical look, skeptical that two invisible backpacks were coincidentally right next to each other. Due to the depth of the moment, I opted not to inject humor and mention Anne's invisible jet was nearby.

"Mine puts extra downward pressure on my heart," she said.

"You hide it well."

"The problem is, the more I try not to think about it, the more I think about it."

I wanted to fix it, but it was *un*fixable. I remained silent. Her eyes sought something, anything. When she realized I had nothing more to offer, she turned towards the river. I felt like I let her down.

"When sparrows fall," I said, the words escaping before I knew my mind summoned them.

"What?" Her eyes fixed on mine again.

I paused so my mind could give my mouth warning. "The Bible says, 'Not a single sparrow can fall to the ground without your Father knowing it.'"

"What does that have to do with my brother? Are you saying it was part of God's plan? If so, please don't go there. It only makes me angrier. At least once a day I've been asking *are you there God? It's me, Mae.* No response yet. My religious beliefs are far from grounded at the moment. In fact, if there is a God, I'm pissed off at Him."

"That's not quite what I meant," I said. "I assume you've been asking yourself *why*, nonstop, until your head is spinning. And…if I have no right to make assumptions on this topic and you want me to shut up now, I will."

"No, it's okay. And, yes, I'm constantly asking *why* this happened, and *what* I could have done to stop it. And it's not getting me anywhere. If anything, it's making things worse. There are no answers. There is no closure."

"Maybe you're asking the wrong questions."

She looked at me like I was clueless. "What do you mean?"

I continued across this precarious bridge, "I mean, instead of *why* and *what*, maybe you should be asking *who?*"

A defense mechanism tripped and her face tightened. "I know *who*," she said. "He did it himself with a fucking belt and hanger rod."

I tried to defuse, "I didn't mean your brother. I'm talking about someone who loves your brother more than you could ever imagine; someone who was waiting to comfort him and heal his pain. The Bible says, 'What is the price of two sparrows—one copper coin? But not a single sparrow can fall to the ground without your Father knowing it. And the very hairs on your head are all numbered. So don't be afraid; you are more valuable to God than a whole flock of sparrows.'

"While you probably feel hopelessly vulnerable," I continued, "at the bottom of this big hole with a total stranger, your brother's completely at peace with where he's at and who he's with. He's free from pain. And he's with someone who doesn't care *why*. He's with someone now who has welcomed him and will love him, period."

Clouds too small to eclipse the sun cut rapidly in front of it, creating a strobe effect on our beach, arresting the moment. A smile fought a valiant battle to conquer her face. The unfiltered light returned, and as her thick lashes rose and dimples bloomed, my heart grew to what felt like a dangerous size.

"Wow," she said. "You're the first person to say something that kind of makes me feel close to okay. And whether I believe it or not, I can tell you believe it. Thank you."

"You're welcome."

Her stare returned to the Colorado.

"You want to hear something really fucked up?" she asked.

"What?"

"My family can't even grieve together. My parents have built a wall so thick and high between them, they won't even embrace, or share memories of their lost child they brought into this world together."

"That's messed up."

"Maybe my brother thought in some sick way it would bring the family back together. Sorry, bro, didn't play out that way." She exhaled the remaining fumes of good will I shared and continued to stare vacantly at the uninterrupted flow.

"Kevin, even if he's in loving company in this safe haven you're talking about, it doesn't help fill the void left in *my* life. Now *I'm* the broken one. *I'm* in pain and questioning *my* own existence."

"I can't begin to understand what that void feels like," I said. "It's…permanent. Though, I imagine you'll slowly build your life back up with enough to keep your mind off it."

"You mean distractions."

"Not really. Distractions are only temporary. I mean more meaningful stuff. Stuff that balances you out so you can reflect on the sadness from a positive place."

"You make it sound so simple," she said.

"I'm sure it's not," I said. "I've never been where you are. This is probably the worst advice in the world."

She smiled. "Life sure isn't easy."

"No, it's not supposed to be," I said. "In fact, that's about the only guarantee we're given during our time on Earth, so I'm happy I'm not living it alone."

"The faith thing again?" she asked.

"You say that like it's a fairy tale," I said. "You do realize His life is documented. I don't think I could recover from all of life's disappointments if I didn't know He was always there to pick me up."

"And you're a saint?"

"Far from it. I get drunk, experiment with drugs, and don't believe sex requires a marriage license. But I *believe*, which outweighs that stuff."

She slowly stood up, and faced me. She blocked out the sun and river. "Tell me, Kevin, why does it have to always be God picking people up? In any relationship, especially marriages, isn't that what your lover is supposed to do?"

"Lover?" I asked.

"What do you call it?"

"I don't know. I suppose *partner* or *companion*. Maybe *mate*."

"*Partner?* Is that what you're seeking in life?" She looked at me sardonically as she jutted her left hip out and put her hand on it. "It's not a business deal. And *companion* is your dog or someone to keep you from feeling lonely. *Mate* is closer but one-dimensional. A one-night stand is technically a *mate*. *Lover* is exactly the right word; someone who *loves* you with an intense, unconditional passion. That's what I'm looking for." She was getting testy.

"Point taken."

"So back to my question," she said. "Why can't your lover provide what you need in life?"

"I suppose they could try, but…"

"But what?" she asked impatiently.

"God has an ability to love and support that we're not able to duplicate. We can aspire to be *like* Him, we just can't *be* Him."

"So you're saying you can't deliver the highest level of love possible? Not high enough to take care of someone, a lover, a family, on your own?" She was on the attack.

"I can deliver the highest level I'm personally capable of."

"But it's not enough?"

"I guess not."

"Sounds like a recipe for failure to me," she said, and waltzed across the beach; she was insinuating our conversation had no grounding. I did not know how to react to her mocking my beliefs. I sensed this was shrapnel from her own difficult battles.

She waltzed back and continued, "I've never heard a priest interrupt wedding vows, 'to have and to hold, from this day forward, for better, for worse, for richer, for poorer, in sickness and in health…*actually, none of that stuff matters a lick because the church has got your back.'"*

"Mae, I'm not saying God's love makes my love unnecessary."

"But you said His is a level we're not able to duplicate. Sounds damn good to me. I think we should kick back, roll with the punches, take the bad with the good, leave it all in His hands, and," she broke into song, *"bet your bottom dollar that tomorrow | there'll fucking be sun.* Right, prophet Kevin? Is that what you see in your crystal ball: *sunshine, lollipops, and rainbows?"*

Mae displayed a prideful look, as if she scored well with an opposition rebuttal. She sat wearily back down in the sand and looked out vacantly. Somehow my attempt to help transitioned to a personal counterattack—exactly why I often avoided this topic. I stood up and offered her a hand. I was invisible and she didn't budge. I recognized her empty expression. It was failure. She had looked into her future and accepted defeat before living it. I was not taught to walk away from someone in this condition.

I proceeded cautiously, choosing every word with purpose, "Mae, we both agree life is hard—*incredibly* hard. And some will have chapters far worse than we ever thought could be written. It sucks, but it's an unavoidable fact. I don't accept this willingly. I'm constantly asking *why*, like you…"

Her head turned upstream. I had caught her attention and she wanted my words to flow directly into her ear. The inevitable afternoon shade from the canyon walls crept across our beach, swallowing her right foot.

I continued, "…but I'm also constantly asking *who? Whose* image was I created in? *Who* is this figure capable of being a perfect and selfless teacher and life coach? *Whom* do I want to model my behavior after to love my family and the greater world around us *intensely* and *unconditionally?"*

The shadow had now enveloped her whole body and was on the verge of sucking me into it. I took a few steps to my left to stay illuminated, reversing the roles. She rotated ever so slightly so she could face my words. Her eyes were neutral and slightly down, suggesting internal processing.

"Mae, you can try to take on this difficult thing called life all by yourself," I said. "You could also meet someone else, equally confused, and try to figure it out together. Or, you could accept an open invitation into a never-ending perpetual intimate relationship with someone who's always looking out for you. And *then* you could pick a lover who wants to support you in the same way. Honestly, I don't think I can be whole, and am set up for failure, if I don't have an intimate relationship with *both* God and my lover."

She continued to look down, and remained silent. The shadow engulfed me. I was about to suggest we head back when she slowly stood up and brushed the sand off the back of her cutoffs. When she raised her head I was rewarded with the deepening of dimples.

"That kind of sounded like a proposal," she said. "Were you promoting faith or yourself?"

"Faith," I said.

"Are you sure? Isn't it a package deal?"

I should be bold. Remember, post-graduation, aggressive, goal-oriented attitude. If you want this, let it be known. "Okay, I think both would be good for you."

"Well, we have known each other one whole day. And I suppose you do owe me your life since I saved it. Can I have time to think about it?" She was kidding on the surface, but I had no idea what was occurring on subconscious levels.

"This offer is only valid in the Grand Canyon," I said, and smiled. "Mae, one final thing. There's a phrase you can think about when you feel out of control."

"Which is?"

"Do you remember the character Montana Wildhack in *Slaughterhouse-Five?*"

"I think so."

"Well, she wore a locket containing what's called the serenity prayer: *God, grant me the serenity to accept the things I cannot change, the courage to change the things I can, and the wisdom to know the difference.*"

"I like that," she said. Her dimples became bottomless. "Kevin, can you please turn around?"

"What?"

"I said turn around."

"Why?"

"Just do it."

"Fine." I turned and faced the canyon wall. I heard water splash. A smirk crossed my face at the first instinctual thought.

"Skinny-dipping?" I said loudly.

"Is that seriously what you're thinking?" she said. "I was so blown away by your inspirational preaching that I eagerly stripped my clothes off so we could ravage each other in the freezing Colorado, in plain view of all of the rafting companies?"

Apparently, I guessed wrong.

"This is insanely cold," she said.

"What are you doing?"

"Trying to relax enough to piss in the river. Don't turn around, my cutoffs and suit bottoms are around my ankles."

My mind overrode a twitching neck muscle. "Be careful. You wouldn't want to fall in above the rapid." I heard her tributary.

"About time," she said. "I held it through your entire gospel."

While my mind was on the other side of the river looking across at her bare butt, I heard a splash, followed by *shit!* I spun around to see her treading water a couple feet from shore.

"What happened?" I asked.

"I fell. Turn around, my pants aren't up."

"I can't see through the water."

"Turn around!"

I obeyed and waited. The silence lasted too long.

"Mae?"

No response.

"Mae?"

Still quiet.

"MAE?" I turned around with feigned-shut eyes and saw her thrashing about in the water a few feet from shore.

Apparently, the risk of being found dead *and* naked below the waist was of greater concern to Mae than the risk of drowning. Her head kept submerging as she expended all of her effort pulling up her suit bottoms and tight cutoffs instead of swimming back to shore. All the while, the hidden underwater current slyly pulled her deeper and closer to the Horn Creek rapid. When the stubborn denim finally crested her butt, she began a relaxed, graceful breaststroke, which soon morphed into a stressful, undisciplined freestyle, as the tow of the rapid tightened its grip. She made poor lateral progress while her downstream speed accelerated. The freezing water also took its toll, shallowing her breaths and stunting her strokes. Floating the Horn Creek rapid without a life vest would be a death wish. I ran downstream.

She kept at her freestyle but was now emitting waterlogged *helps* in between strokes. The echo off the canyon walls intensified her desperation. Mae lacked Anne's superhero talents, and her aquatic efforts were futile. An irrational smile spread itself across my face when I thought about all of our misfortune this weekend. It was as if *Fantasy Island*'s Mr. Roarke, definitely not *Love Boat*'s Julie McCoy, was in charge of our itinerary. I quickly disarmed the smile.

I was at a crossroads: run past the rapid and fish her, likely dead, out at the bottom, or pretend I was the *Six Million Dollar* Steve Austin, dive in, swim like mad to Mae, and attempt to stay alive and guide her to safety. I had given her a fire and brimstone speech about aspiring to model myself after the ultimate advocate. What would He do? Didn't recall Him ever swimming. He was always parting, walking on, or dunking people in, the stuff. Art Garfunkel recycled in my head, *like a bridge over troubled water* |

I will lay me down. Interesting choice of His, using Art to help me decide.

After shedding my shirt and boots and making an overly dramatic dive, I gasped when I pierced the freezing water and my ribcage and lungs contracted. When I surfaced, shivering, I had trouble sucking in a full breath and wore a tight imaginary neck brace. My heart raced. Instinctively, I grunted to expand my lungs and began swimming before accepting these new sensations as reality. My muscles were tense and my freestyle erratic.

After every couple strokes I looked up to get my bearings. Being on the same plane with Mae made it difficult to keep her in sight. The noise of the river added to the confusion and an ice cream headache set in. It appeared Mae had given up on swimming and was now passively floating towards her fate. I thought about how her brother had found a way to escape his pain. Was the prospect of drowning not an unattractive one to Mae? I did not recall her taking off her invisible backpack before entering the water. Crap! I forgot to take mine off, too.

I realized there was no way I was going to reach Mae before the rapid. I shouted for her to switch to a backside feet first position. She faced downstream and I had no idea if she could hear. Since my fate was now also sealed, I continued swimming towards her, purposefully accelerating towards certain doom.

I trailed Mae by ten yards as she passed between the horns. She was instantly pulled under and out of sight. I knew it was the last time I would ever see her. I knew it was the last time I would ever see *anybody*. Our bloated, lifeless bodies would be reunited wherever driftwood pooled. I had about five more seconds of air, 5...4...3...2...1...I swallowed water in complete darkness.

My arms flailed in an attempt to find one of the 25,000 imaginary basketballs to hold on to. I tensed in anticipation of slamming against invisible rocks. My lips sealed tight to protect teeth and to stop imbibing river. My forehead, knees, and elbows practiced feeling the pain in anticipation of impact. I kept my eyes open to help equilibrium, though I was blinded and experienced the sensation of ice cubes glued to my corneas. The backside feet first position involuntarily switched to side with butt first, stomach with arms first, back with face first, and countless other horrific alignments. I bumped a few rocks, but the cold numbed the pain and masked the damage level. The whole time—*under.* My saving grace that I learned from surfing was that I was usually much closer to the surface than I thought, and I would naturally come up after the rough water had passed. Only, this was a hundred-yard path of rough water, and there were random hazards to get wedged in or knocked against.

My chest tightened, eyes bulged, and head fogged as the need for air accelerated. I could not believe I was the cliché daft tourist who died trying to save another—whom I'd known only *one* day. I was dying *voluntarily*. After our bodies were found, the article would read, *they were last seen singing on the shore of the Colorado River. Hallucinogenic drugs, popular with today's youth, have not been ruled out.* I'm not ready for this. I almost died yesterday. This was the most fucked up second chance ever. My head filled with flashes of light. Oh, shit, I really needed air.

My left ear popped with a sharp pain when it unexpectedly broke the surface. It sounded like a radio's volume turned up all the way, in between stations. I turned my mouth in the same direction and, with a resounding guttural cry, found the wonderful substance it was designed to inhale. Instantaneously, I went under again. The current's grip loosened enough to where I could resume a safer backside feet first position. My face partially surfaced again and the sun burned my eyes. I produced more guttural orchestrations as I dropped my legs down and surfaced my whole head as a periscope.

The noise was deafening and it was hard to generate thoughts. Where was Mae, and how far was I from shore? The queries of selflessness and survival were equals. I could not see Mae, but I gauged I was twenty-five feet from the familiar side of the river. Our concert stage was just up ahead. I was still in the most violent part of this ride.

I suddenly remembered Pinto's rock, threw my arms back and tucked my feet as high as possible. My soles surfed over a large object and I avoided a crippling blow. I arched my back and braced my hands under my butt, riding the Wham-O Slip 'N Slide until I dumped over the precipice and submerged deep into the dark swirling eddy below. I attempted to surface, but water cascaded over the precipice and pounded me down, making it feel like I was not just under, but being held under. I tried to stroke in the direction I felt was downstream, away from the rock, but the recirculating flow was too strong. Even though I had breathed air moments ago, I was still in a deficit and my need for it resumed accelerating.

Through surfing, I had experience in rip currents, strong channels of water flowing seaward. Swimming against them was fruitless, so you had to exit out the sides. I had to try to break the eddyline the same way. Utilizing underwater breaststroke, I aimed beyond the edge of the precipice whitewater. My left shoulder painfully collided with an object in the way. Unlike bumping into a rock, *it* moved when I hit it. I reached out with my left hand and tried to use my lone remaining sense, touch, to figure out what it was. My fingers inconclusively slipped off. It *could* be Mae. My need for air was hastened. Pressure pushed my head inside out, my thoughts blurred, and lights flashed. I had time for only one more escape attempt, regardless of whether I tried pushing this thing along with me. As I propelled my body against the foreign object, my left hand got tangled in something. I viciously tried to relocate water behind me with frog kicks and my free right arm. My chest and head were exploding.

Translucent water materialized as I neared the surface, and with a strong kick I burst through—the fresh air tore painfully through my collapsed lungs. The spray in my face confirmed I was only a foot to the side of the eddy, sure to get sucked right back in, and next to me was Mae's body, my left hand trapped under her bikini strap against her back. The noise, spray, and return pull of the eddy were too distracting for me to assess her condition, but her face was fully submerged. I gripped her strap with my right hand and retracted my left. I threw my back and left arm in a high barrel roll arc away from the eddy. For the first time in my life, and polar opposite of when John Blutarsky was on top of the ladder, I prayed for that strap not to unclasp. I sidestroked with my left arm and frog-kicked until I broke through the eddyline and reentered the main rapid flow, with Mae in tow.

I did not get sucked under this time, perhaps because our two connected bodies were more raft-like. When I gathered my wits, I realized Mae was not moving, beyond floating, and was still face down. I rolled her face up and spooned her on top of my front, both of us backside feet first. I held her with my left arm while I kept my right arm free for steering and pushing off. Her extra weight sunk my butt to depths that punished it with multiple contusions. Mae's head was limp, eyes closed, and if she was breathing, it was not noticeable. I was yelling her name and smacking her face. I wanted to check her pulse but my hands were too numb.

Aside from sporadic temporary dunks, collecting more bruises, and the mental torture of knowing Mae was likely dead in my arms and there was nothing I could do about it, the remaining rapid did not feel as life-threatening. More consistent breaths and the desire to get Mae to a stable place sharpened my decision-making. I steered and paddled us to a safe beach, a hundred yards downstream of our stage. All the while I had been indexing my mental medical catalogue, seeking a similar situation *Emergency*'s Gage and Desoto, *M*A*S*H*'s Hawkeye, *Trek*'s Bones, *Love Boat*'s Bricker, or even *Quincy* himself, might have encountered.

I dragged Mae out of the water and laid her on her back in the fully shaded sand. My shivering intensified from the full air exposure and my speech was stuttered. Mae was not shivering at all. Nor was her chest cresting. I tilted her head back, opened her mouth wide, put my ear to it, and…a gallon of Colorado River geysered upward with great force. I rolled her to her side so anything coming out would stay out. It was a lot. The geysering was followed by a fit of deep coughs. When the sounds tapered, I put my hand on her shoulder.

"Leave me alone," she slurred.

"Mae, let me help."

She attempted to stand on her own and fell forward. I tried to stabilize her.

"I said, leave me alone," she said, and shoved my shivering hand away. Her skin felt cool as ice like mine, but her body was calm. She stood up on her own this time and looked around. She turned towards the river, paused, and then walked towards it.

"Mae, what the fuck are you doing?" I said, and blocked her path.

She pushed me out of the way. I wrapped my arms around her from behind, locking her arms at her sides. I thought I'd read somewhere that hypothermia could play with your mind. The only treatment I could think of was warmth. She kicked and screamed as I carried her towards a nearby patch of tall grass, the only remaining sunny spot in our vicinity. I flanked her down on the ground and my grip was the rope keeping her from escaping. After a few minutes of screaming and struggling, she submitted and lay still. I did not know whether it was the sunlight, struggle, or skin-on-skin contact, but my shivering stopped. Ironically, hers started. I kept my grasp locked, and as our spot shaded over, I passed out from exhaustion.

18. '01

M ae was not in the lounge when I returned from ice-skating with my Cutlass. I asked the Farrah Fawcett–feathered-hair gal at the front desk whether she saw her leave, specifically *with* her luggage. It was an irrational, yet honest, question. She had not. I found her asleep on our bed, fully clothed with an open Bible in her lap. Her closed eyes looked youthful and unscathed from any recent grieving. She must have found a comforting verse.

I was responsible for introducing Mae to this, her favorite book. She became fascinated at the wealth of life lessons it contained. She was especially fond of the parables, marveling at how simple examples could tackle such weighty subjects.

When Mae and I struggled early on in our marriage from differing approaches to conflict resolution, we sought help from a marriage counselor at our church. His primary piece of advice had been to study the Bible together. Mae was eager and I happily endorsed the approach since I had already mastered the subject, or so I had thought. I dusted off the heavily dog-eared copy from my youth. Unlike me, Mae dove into the granular dissection of verses with the same passion she applied to everything. I learned a few new things but still felt the *overall picture* was the most important concept to grasp. Her details and examples were countered by my frequently irrelevant generic responses, which exposed my feigned interest. My participation eventually became a hindrance to her studying, so I politely removed myself from the process. She told me this decision was immeasurably more disappointing to her than any of our arguments, especially since these were the ideals I had courted her with.

Unfortunately, this began a repeating pattern of crossroads, seeking guidance, vowing practice and change, tapering off, and inevitable backsliding. We were both guilty of not executing, but it was my fixed mindset that ultimately always defeated her one of growth. I got away with it every time, but I feared now we weren't at a new crossroads—we were at a dead-end.

I should have woken her. This was the ideal, tranquil setting to calmly open our imperative dialogue. I didn't. It was truly sad how the topic of our marriage had become a polarizing one, inspiring avoidance *instead* of engagement, similar to discussions of faith with non-believers. I wrote a note on the nightstand and left. It was the cowardly move, even though I knew the rug I kept sweeping things under was threadbare and unraveling fast.

I pulled up a seat at the bar in the smoke-filled El Tovar Lounge and Tom, member of the new Willie Aames trio, poured me a Lite and gave me a bowl of Dixies Drumstick crackers. A few seats over someone was asleep on the counter, possibly passed out. My dad's businessman haircut took the seat across from me in the mirrored backing. The Little River Band lectured, *you have to face up, you can't run and hide | have you heard about the lonesome loser,* from speakers above. The prisoner's view out the window had not changed. The place was packed—alcohol nicely complemented bad weather. Multiple families had set their kids up with board games on the cocktail tables while they drank their afternoon boredom away. I envied the kids' innate desire to compete against their siblings. I recognized the green houses and red hotels of *Monopoly,* the savings and loan interest chart of *Payday,* and the silver drill rigs of *King Oil.* The kids were treated to unlimited Cokes and second-hand smoke. Tom informed me Willie Aames was coming in later and we needed to get the band back together.

Ranger Ponch entered the lounge and sat down in the seat to my left. He put an odd-looking motorcycle helmet on the counter.

"Work slow?" Tom asked him.

"Nobody's walking the rim today," he said. "You can't see a thing in this weather. I miss the moderate winters from my Phantom Ranch days. Piña colada, please."

I turned to him and said, "I think you worked down at Phantom Ranch when my friends and I came here in the late seventies."

"Yeah, that was probably me. They prefer to keep younger rangers down there, so my partner and I got moved up to the rim years ago."

"That's an interesting helmet you have," I said. The front sixty degrees of the gold half-dome helmet was royal blue with a gold decal of an eagle flying through a circle.

"Thanks, man. It's a replica from that old TV show, *CHiPs.* Some people think I look like that character, Ponch, so I use it as a conversation piece with the ladies. I don't actually ride."

"Does it work?"

"Hit and miss." He looked dejected. "Your copter tours still grounded?" he asked Tom.

"Yep," Tom said. "Not that there'd be any customers in this weather."

"I didn't know you were a helicopter pilot," I said. "How exciting."

"I suppose," he said. "Flying tourists for twenty-two years on the *same* routes in the *same* copter and *still* needing to bartend to pay the bills."

He poured himself a few ounces of whiskey and shot it. Were bartenders supposed to drink? He didn't appear interested in expanding on his career, so I turned back to the fake motorcycle cop.

"What kind of crazy stuff have you seen working here?"

"I've never seen anyone fall, though that's what I get asked the most," he said, eating the pineapple chunk off the plastic sword in his drink.

"The funniest moments happened in one of my early years," he continued. "It was right after the Duke died. I was working down in Phantom when my walkie-talkie went crazy one morning. At first I thought the ranger from Indian Garden was crying and making a distress call, but it turned out he was crying from laughing so hard. Two shirtless fruits, hand in hand, with extra tight cord shorts, were skipping and singing down the Bright Angel trail to the soundtrack of *Grease*."

I froze. Creative liberties were being taken with an event I knew intimately.

He continued, "They were sprinkling flower petals, making out, and grabbing each other's crotches..."

"Bullshit," I interrupted. "They wore shirts and normal cord shorts. And they weren't skipping or sprinkling flowers, and sure as hell weren't making out or crotch grabbing. And only *one* of them was singing."

Tom and the ranger stared at me blank-faced, trying to figure out why my response was so angry and passionate.

"How would you know?" the ranger asked.

My mind raced for an explanation. "Another ranger told me the same story earlier."

He seemed to accept this implausible answer.

"So, the next day," the ranger said, proceeding with caution, "A chick came running through Phantom Ranch claiming she had discovered a Neanderthal man. She was followed by a guy caked from head to toe in red mud. He was naked with the exception of some type of makeshift sling to attempt to cover his dick, which it didn't. It was the funniest thing I've ever seen. Poor guy, though. He had gotten caught in a flash flood in Phantom Creek and was lucky to be alive."

I was smiling. Tom and the ranger were looking to me to see if I was going to critique this story also. Coincidentally, I knew this one, too. I had told a much longer version as part of my best man's speech at my friend Chad's wedding.

"Well, that story is completely true," I commented, "because he's my best friend and I was there."

"Seriously? What a small world," the ranger said with a big grin.

"How long have you been a park ranger?" I asked.

"Twenty-five years. Twenty-five *fucking* years." I sensed a disappointment similar to Tom's.

"You must enjoy it," I said.

"I do. Millions of people come to see this place—half of them ladies. I've slept with one from every state and just about every country."

"Dyn-o-mite!" said Tom.

"So that's why you keep doing it?" I asked the ranger. "To save on travel expenses?"

"Funny. No. I keep doing it because I'm waiting to meet *the* one, like my partner did. He's got a great gal, two delightful kids I'm a godfather to, and a nice home in Williams. Living the dream."

"I see you're married," he said, and pointed to my ring. "Where did you and your wife meet?"

"The...Grand Canyon," I said guiltily. "How do you know it'll be here and not somewhere else?"

"Because a relationship born in the Grand Canyon is something special. The common thing *all* visitors seem to be looking for here, besides the big pit you currently can't see, is meaning. Locals call it *finding grand*. People aspire to use the big void to fill holes in their own lives. Watch their eyes as they pause at the rim's edge to take in the view—minds go into overdrive on what they want out of life."

"Why do you think that is?" I asked.

"I think seeing it gives people faith," he said, "that if something so beautiful can be created out of rock, then think of what can be done with them."

"Problem is, most people don't have a clue what their *grand* is," Tom said. "I haven't figured it out in all of my years here."

"It's probably different for each person," the ranger said. "And I suppose it could change over time."

"Hard to hit a moving target," Tom said.

Our casual afternoon saloon philosophy carried a lot more weight than likely intended, and time froze as I processed the personal application.

"Maybe they're all searching for the same thing and just don't know it. And maybe they already have it," I said.

"Friend, don't start spreading that rumor. It'll hurt tourism," Tom said, and threw back another shot of whiskey.

"But you met your wife here," the ranger said to me. "You found something."

"Yes," I said, "but I didn't come here looking for her. We met by chance. And it's a little depressing to think my life would be meaningless if I had never met her."

"Would it be?" Tom asked.

"I don't know. Maybe," I said.

"So you met by chance your first time here," the ranger said. "Why did you come back this time?"

I was about to confess when the drunk at the end of the counter roared to life, "I met my wife here, too." He was a skinny guy, about my age, with a dopey grin. To the chorus of Foreigner's "Double Vision," he reached for the half-empty draft in front of him that Tom had taken away long ago.

"Another?" he asked Tom.

"I think you've had enough for now," Tom said.

"You're probably right," he slurred. "Anyway, I met the person who *should* be my wife here, but I blew my chance. She'll come back someday, though. I'll get another chance. They *all* come back to the canyon."

My curiosity was piqued. "What happened?"

"I was guiding my first ever rafting trip down the Colorado. Another guide and I pulled our boats over above a rapid to scout it out. There was a gal there on the shore who could have been sisters with Linda Blair, the older *Roller Boogie* version, not the young *Exorcist* one. I can still picture her green bikini top. She was outta sight. We immediately hit it off because we shared a passion for environmentalism. She was with some square-looking dude, so it would have been awkward asking for her number, but I knew she wanted to give it to me." He paused, lost in thought or drunkenness.

His memory had stimulated activity in my brain and I was trying to process why.

"And?" the ranger asked him.

Startled, the drunk continued, "I had my 8-track player in the boat and she made a song request for when we shot the rapid. She ended up singing loudly along with it, like a serenade, as I brought my raft through. I intentionally got the raft stuck in an eddy right in front of her so we could check each other out more. And when we broke out of the eddy, she flipped up her bikini top and showed me the most beautiful set of breasts ever created—two Eden apples. Yeah, baby!" He lost his train of thought again.

My mind was in overdrive.

"Then what?" Tom asked him.

"Then I guided my crew to the bottom of the rapid and waited for my friend's boat, in case he had any swimmers I had to fish out. I was planning on parking and running back up shore to her, but some square tourist spilled out of my friend's boat and the current swept us downstream as we picked her up. I never saw the green bikini gal again, but I know she was *the* one."

"What song was she singing?" I asked.

He thought for a moment. "I think it was the Sex Pistols' 'Anarchy in the U.K.'"

"Friend," the ranger said to him, while pointing to the lounge entrance, "There's a pretty lady who looks like Linda Blair."

As I spotted Mae, and the crests of her Eden apples in her golden U of A fleece, everything clicked. As she walked over to us and the drunk turned around to see, I hastily jumped off my seat, threw a few bills on the bar, thanked Tom, said goodbye to the ranger, told the drunk I was damn glad to meet him, then caught Mae's arm in mine and guided her, confused, back into the lobby.

"I thought we were grabbing drinks," she said.

"No. It's getting claustrophobic in here. Let's go someplace else."

I steered her to the front doors that once welcomed Theodore Roosevelt and Albert Einstein. We passed Willie Aames, not as celebrated as Teddy or Al, who was on his way in.

"Hey, are we singing tonight?" Willie Aames asked me.

Behind us the drunk stumbled out of the lounge and yelled, "You came back. I've been waiting all of these years."

Mae asked me, "Is that guy talking to Willie Aames?"

"Must be," I said, and pushed her towards the exit. I looked back just in time to see the drunk slip on the spinning wheel of a *Life* board game two kids were playing on the ground and fall flat on his back. Sorry, Pinto.

19. '79

I awoke to a perfectly still canyon, frozen by the flat light of early summer evening. Though an auditory illusion, the river noise softened in tune with my relaxed breathing. Lying on my back, with an inside-out view of the beauty of patient erosion, I felt like I was looking outward from a coffee table book. I ached all over.

On her side, looking at me, Mae traced paths on my face with her finger. Not reading into this because my brain was still turned off, it took me a few flashes to recollect the hellish events that had led up to this serene moment.

When our eyes met, her curiosity confirmed she retained even less than I did, "What happened?"

After I told the tale, which included multiple stops and starts where I questioned my accuracy and lucidity, Mae stared at me in awe. I was in disbelief myself.

"You *happened* to bump into me?" she asked.

"Basically."

"And almost died yourself?"

"Yes."

"I should be dead right now," she said.

"No, you shouldn't."

"*Yes*, I should!"

"But you're not."

"Only thanks to you."

"I got lucky."

"Lucky? There was no luck involved in this."

I concurred, "No, there wasn't. Someone was looking out for both of us. It was my turn to save you, though."

"Is that why you jumped in? To pay off a debt?"

I pondered. "No. I wanted you to live."

"Thank you," she said.

I stared up again at the sky in a daze, smiling and musing at how harrowing of an experience it was. "You're welcome."

"No!" she said, and used her hand to firmly turn my head towards her so our eyes locked. She paused and gave me a harsh look, without a dimple or line in sight. "I'm thanking you for my life." Her delivery and tone were parochial school strict. The words were thick, bold font with heavy trailing shadows. She achieved her goal of weighing down this conversation to sink it to the depths of the subject matter.

Muscle memory held me under again, collapsing my lungs as I managed to gasp out, "You're welcome."

Her breathing quickened and she searched intensely in my eyes, scared, not anxious, but cruelly, inconsolably alone and disoriented, looking for a glint of the future I claimed I could offer. Through the portal opened between us I could see she was hanging on to hope by a mere thread while despair had already fully welcomed her, comforted her, and promised to always be there for her. My mind seized the thread and formed a hazy revelation; one I was not able to bring into focus, but one that was a few rows higher up on her eye chart based on the infinitesimal recognition she registered. Her eyes widened and face glowed as whatever she glimpsed fostered her hope, arrested her despair, and provided comfort.

My eyes, not hers, broke first from the strain of trying to save someone with only a glance. Appreciating the intensity of my labors and resolve, her eyes yielded and allowed her soul to escape over to my haven, and then they closed to dam despair's vicious efforts to hold her back. When they reopened they displayed a hard-fought innocence, accompanied by relaxed, peaceful breathing. The storm followed the calm and her eyes welled up and spilled over. I protectively wrapped my arms around her and held tight. I felt responsible for her. It felt good. It felt *right*.

Her face was cradled between my shoulder and chin. In between sobs, I felt her warm breath on my neck. As the sobs retreated, her breathing slowed, the warmth intensified, and my senses heightened. Tiny pecks tasted my neck, then her lips parted for the tongue to join in, and her mouth slid a route along my jawline. When our lips met, I felt worlds apart from some guy she supposedly kissed out of curiosity last night. There was an exchange that could only be sourced from powerful, volatile, and dangerous depths. Circumstances had circumnavigated several relationship levels, and I did not feel like her *partner, companion*, or *mate*—I felt like…her *lover*.

She pulled her head away. "Are you humming 'Feels Like the First Time'?"

Was I? Oh, crap, I was. Seriously, Kevin? I felt so unbelievably good with her that it came out organically. "I'll stop."

When our advances progressed to the inevitable awkward point, I tried to make light of it, "I didn't put one of those things in my pack because I was afraid of the extra weight."

"Don't worry. I'm on the pill," she said.

"I thought you said *life needs to be dealt with naturally*."

"What's more natural than fucking?"

With that well-articulated thesis, nothing more needed to be said on the matter. There was no one around, but when she positioned herself on top of me, for security her bikini top remained the sole piece of clothing between us. While I stared up at her entrancing lashes, with her river-tumbled hair cascading toward me, *it* radiated out of her again. The glow grew into a blinding force. I was mesmerized, squinting at the edges, which extended a good few inches around her whole body. And even though I killed the hum, the Foreigner lyrics flooded my head, *I have waited a lifetime | spent my time so foolishly | but now that I've found you | together we'll make history.*

"This is the most awe-inspiring view I've ever seen," I said.

Mae thought I was staring over her shoulder and she craned her head back and looked up at the majesty of the canyon walls. "Oh my. The canyon does look amazing." She looked down at me again.

"What canyon?" I said, holding her gaze.

Her dimples cratered as her cheeks swelled. I would wait until we were done to mention she lost her tooth in the river.

20. '01

Mae drove since I had too much Miller in my tank. The snow-packed slick roads were imprinted with tracks from other vehicles attempting an escape. An endless sea of white spread across our view, and the undersides of pines were the only exposed color. The snowfall paused, the sky was a detail-less gray, and an eye-level fog, like someone's vague thoughts, required headlights and kept our speed to a minimum. It seemed everything we did recently was in slow motion since we were in no rush to get where we were headed. The cranked heater turned the Cutlass into a sauna. Mae popped in Nick Drake, a clinically depressed young English singer who died from an overdose in the mid-seventies. His tragic life made Mae a big fan, and his dreamy, yet gloomy, music matched the weather.

I had no preconceived destination. The scenic rim roads to the west and east were both closed due to the weather. Only the park entrance/exit road was open, so I suggested we head out and poke around the nearby town of Tusayan, a mostly lodging community for canyon tourists. As we headed out the gates, nonexistent incoming traffic was being welcomed by one lone operating booth. The Richard Dreyfuss with sideburns lookalike ranger stood outside the booth constructing a Devils Tower replica out of snow, and gave us an *I told you so* look as we passed.

Tusayan was only minutes away, but we immediately ran into a Christmas tree string of brake lights. Mae precariously veered to the side of the road while braking and we saw an accident scene ahead. Either the fear of being trapped with me for an undetermined period in a cramped space, or a relentless pent-up desire to go against the grain, caused Mae to right-turn off the main road onto a side street, piercing the Kaibab National Forest.

The encroaching snow on the sides of the unplowed road made it only one-and-a-half lanes wide, and an oncoming car would require one driver to yield. It was a residential area with small homes and low-end apartment buildings, likely for the transient hotel employees made up of drifters and foreign youths with temporary visas. Ideally it would be a back road into Tusayan, but since we had no proof, I readied a risk-averse protest. Then I remembered how one misstep could be your last on a precipice, so I silenced my conservatism. Instead, I did my best John Denver and crooned, to Mae's amusement, *country roads, take me home | to the place I belong.*

The random road took us deeper into the forest, where there were no addresses. It reminded me of the empty rural roads near the San Diego Wild Animal Park where I taught Warren and Hazel how to drive. I glanced over at Mae's pencil tip chin scar, and then her slightly parted lips. Over the years, while the rest of her teeth naturally yellowed, her porcelain implant remained its original shiny white. She recently replaced it with a more weathered one. It was an odd thought, making something intentionally imperfect. I knew if I thought hard enough there would be a lesson in it somewhere.

In contrast, looking at my sun-damaged maroon dashboard and the busted seams of my maroon pillow-topped swivel bucket seats, I wondered why I held on to this car for so long. I once saw a Cutlass magazine ad with a girl in a bikini facing outward on the swivel seat. Perhaps I felt I would not get a full return on my $2,900 purchase until Mae twisted around on the velour in swimwear?

"Your new tooth looks a lot better," I said.

"Thanks," she said through monkey-like protruding lips, to give me a better view.

"I think you look better without it, though," I said.

She smiled. "I still can't believe you didn't tell me right away it was gone that day."

"I didn't want to ruin the moment. It might have changed *everything.*"

Her furrowed brow suggested I accidentally stimulated deep thought. She went silent, with eyes forward on the barren road. She did this a lot. I used to think it was solely attributable to re-membering her brother and trying to numb herself against the return of the pain. Now it felt like there were multiple focuses feed-ing her states of withdrawal. I would be implausibly ignorant to believe I was not one of them.

When she snapped out of it, she half-smiled and said, "What is the price of two sparrows—one copper coin? But not a single spar-row can fall to the ground without your Father knowing it. And the very hairs on your head are all numbered. So don't be afraid; you are more valuable to God than a whole flock of sparrows."

"I like that," I said. "It's in the Bible, right?"

Her half-smile lost the half. "It's Matthew 10:29 to 31. You don't remember that passage?"

"I think I do," I said hesitantly.

Mae shot me a look similar to when we realized I did not have my driver's license at the Tijuana border crossing—on the side with the bacon-wrapped hot dogs. I could not comprehend why she was so annoyed I could not remember *one* passage. Her faith had be-come so strong that I ceded the role of family spiritual leader to her many years ago. Work and kid-focused activities were always easy, low-hanging alternatives and excuses.

A long, continuous fence sprouted up on our left. On the other side of it was the beginning of the two-mile runway of the Grand Canyon Airport, which was just south of the town of Tusayan, meaning we overshot it. As Mae and I looked over at the inactive terminal, control tower, hangars, and the unfortunate planes and helicopters left out in the elements, a painful memory surfaced. I knew Mae either had the same recollection, or was dwelling on the general disappointment that flight, figuratively and literally, had become a divide in our relationship.

I had never been fully cured of the out-of-control feeling I felt when death attempted to pull me backwards over the canyon railing twenty-two years ago. The terror, and invisible backpack, returned to my life many times, especially in airplanes and other locales next to vast nothingness. A few beers could counter it in the early years when Mae and I were frequent flyers, but as I grew older and felt more vulnerable, a lower tolerance required more alcohol, and sometimes an anti-anxiety pill, and I made excuses to avoid flying. Masking and evading, instead of confronting and solving—my default coping method was doing me no favors. Most of our family vacations were road trips, and we got to know the western part of the country intimately. Mae enjoyed herself and didn't complain, but I could tell it was unnatural for her wings to be clipped. In recent years, while she had gone on nearly a dozen international missionary trips, and a handful of eastern college visits with the kids, I had gone on none of either. In fact, it had been over five years since I last stepped foot on a plane.

"It probably reconnects with Route 64 after the airport," Mae said.

I was lost in thought. "What?"

"This should connect with Route 64," she repeated.

I was thinking about the quote from my graduation commencement speech, *nothing on earth can help the man with the wrong mental attitude.* I couldn't postpone this any longer. "Mae, I am so, so, so sorry for *everything.*"

She turned towards me with a very brokenhearted, yet empathetic, look.

"I can't believe I've done all of this to us," I continued.

Ashamed to face her, I turned back to the windshield and my translucent reflection. I now saw so much of my father in me: thicker eyebrows, indifference, narrower eyes, inappreciativeness, higher hairline, selfishness, deeper forehead ruts, cowardliness, and antlers. *The cat's in the cradle and the silver spoon...* Antlers? Antlers? Fuck! I reached over and cranked the steering wheel to the right before Mae even had a chance to react to the herd of mule deer blocking our path. Our rear end fishtailed to the left, and our Cutlass was swinging for the fences at helpless, breathing, motorcycle-sized piñatas. It was going to be a demolition derby, without helmets or Leather Tuscadero's older sister, Pinky.

21. '79

I t was a long, laborious hike back to the ranch for two extremely tired, hungry, thirsty, and awkwardly intimate strangers. I knew in all likelihood it had been a one-day stand, but it simultaneously felt like the culmination of something way beyond young hormones. Mae adjusted gracefully to her new toothless look. She realized there was no immediate solution and therefore no reason to worry. Many girls I had dated wouldn't leave their sorority house if a pimple reached a certain diameter, or, heaven forbid, if there was any snow on the peak. Conversation was light aside from a few name game revivals—Charlie Daniels, David Berkowitz, Bubba Smith, Saddam Hussein (Mae, from her poli-sci class: *untrustworthy new leader of the country of Iraq*).

As we neared our destination, my anxiety grew. Today was one of the best days of my life, except for the part when I witnessed my best friend getting swallowed by a wall of mud, and when I found a love interest lifeless and face down in the Colorado, and, of course, the highly uncomfortable act of almost drowning. Even with all of the near tragic drama, the connection established with Mae had me dreading the day's end. What if our mental collision, complemented by great sex, was merely what Captain Ahab and his *Pequod* crew sought on the high seas—a *fluke?*

As meat-flavored smoke wafted out of the Bright Angel Campground and teased our ravenous appetites, our walk back to reality entered a bizarre phase. Guitar chords, and then male vocals, serenaded us, *I realize the best part of love is the thinnest slice | and it don't count for much | but I'm not letting go | I believe there's still much to believe in.* The melody and lyrics reached us cleanly from an unknown source.

"I bet it's coming from the ranch," Mae said.

The invisible singer continued, *so lift your eyes if you feel you can | reach for a star and I'll show you a plan | I figured it out | what I needed was someone to show me.*

"These lyrics are square," I said. "It must be one of those new soft rock radio stations." At least my fingers were not still intertwined with my frat brother's.

A different sounding, male falsetto took over vocals, *you know you can't fool me | I've been loving you too long | it started so easy | you want to carry on.*

"I think this is live," Mae said. "And I hate to admit it, but I like it."

The two voices joined together, *lost in love and I don't know much | was I thinking aloud and fell out of touch | but I'm back on my feet | and eager to be what you wanted.*

"Who are they covering?" I asked. "Simon and Garfunkel? Loggins and Messina? Seals and Crofts? England Dan and John Ford Coley? Hall and Oates?"

"Did Richard Dawson ask you to name the top seventies male duos?" Mae said.

Although it was as hokey as a junior high love note, even I—despite attempting to increase my testosterone count to fight it off— was being softened up. I felt a strong urge to hold Mae's hand—a relationship assassin when done too early. I kept my thoughts, and hand, to myself. *Shit!* I realized I was smiling like Greg Brady. I tried to extinguish my grin by thinking of his antonym—*Mean Joe* Greene. I observed Mae smirking and wondered if she was hosting as much of a mental struggle. I put on my best poker face through a few more verses and made sure the growing warmth in my heart was chilled at my neckline.

It was dusk as we approached the mule corral. We were steps away from the last turn that would bring us into view of the other Phantom Ranch residents. Shifting campfire light and a repeating chorus of *lost in love* bounced off the canyon walls. *Our* moment was ending. Soon, I would limp along with my *wasn't-meant-to-be* crutch. What would Greg Brady do? What would Mean Joe do? Without a lead-up move, warning, permission, or boundaries, I grabbed Mae's hand and pulled her with me against the corral fence. Her body gracefully collided with mine, like a slinky to a stair, and her parting lips completed the union. A long, intense kiss followed, where my tongue kept trying to penetrate the gap left by her missing incisor, while a barren of mules hee-hawed behind us. We parted, but only for a moment before she pushed me back against the fence and engaged me in an even more passionate embrace that left much of our curious long-faced audience whimpering in jealousy. For a moment I thought we were going to lie in a manger, but when the *lost in love* chorus ended, she abruptly pulled away and hiked solo around the corral corner, leaving me to try to smooth out my now lumpy hiking shorts. I had no idea what I was supposed to read into this. Deep in contemplation, I felt a warm breath against the back of my neck, then leapt away from a mule in heat.

I followed ten yards behind Mae towards a campfire at the center of the ranch. I assumed she was processing and I wanted to be respectful of her physical and mental space. She suddenly stopped, not to wait for me, but to observe a scene between the campfire and us. Ranger Carroll led his wife by hand on to the top of a picnic table. He put his right hand behind her back, and his left hand held her right hand at shoulder-level. Her left hand rested on his shoulder. They slow danced, and the firelight projected giant profiles of them against a canyon wall. Their eyes angled into each other's. She was singing something quietly to him. I stopped next to Mae, who was frozen, mesmerized. I recognized the lilt and lyrics of Doris Day's classic, "Sentimental Journey," coming out of Jeanne's lips. Their whole world was on top of that picnic table, and the audience was not even an afterthought. Before I knew it, I had attempted a relationship assassination and entwined my fingers in Mae's. Her hand contracted and locked us together. I whispered *leave them be* and slowly pulled her away.

There were a dozen guests sitting around the campfire. Chad and Anne sat next to each other on a log, faces beaming, as they listened to two minstrels next to them, the source of our serenaded approach to the ranch, launch into another song. Chad, tinted red from today's mud bath, had the same dumb look he sported during yesterday's handholding episode. His stereo, politely quiet, was nestled at his feet. Disgustingly, his headband, minus most of the stains, was back in place. I could not be sure from afar, but there did not appear to be any space between Anne's prominent right butt cheek and Chad's left. Anne's legs and arms were tattooed with red long sleeves and tube socks.

When Mae and I entered the ring of fire, the minstrels ceased performing as Chad and Anne jumped up to greet us. They had been worried and claimed they were about to organize a search party. There was a pile of smashed beer cans next to their log suggesting otherwise. Chad was quick to point out Mae's new hillbilly smile. He was also grinning at me, assuming our lengthy private time was spent at a *Love Boat* port of call, like Acapulco or Puerto Vallarta, doing what frequent passenger Charo called the *cuchi cuchi*. We described our hellish experience, not confirming the *cuchi cuchi* supposition, and showed them our multiple battle bruises collected as evidence. Thankfully, they each stowed an extra steak dinner plate, which we tore into at the campfire while draining their canteens.

Chad introduced us to his guitar-playing friends, "Do you remember last week's 'Live from Australia' episode of *The Midnight Special*? These guys were on it. Russell, Graham, what's your band's name again? *Air* something?"

"Supply," Russell, short with curly dark hair, said in an Aussie accent.

"Too soft," Chad said. "You've got to toughen it up. How about 'Air Disaster' or 'Pain Supply'?"

"We've already released four albums in Australia," said Graham, tall with blond hair, in the same Aussie accent. "We can't change our name."

"Whatever, dude," Chad said. "Only trying to help. Are you guys done performing? I want to play my tunes."

"I liked that 'lost' song," Mae said.

"Thank you," Russell said, startled by the gap in her mouth. "It's called 'Lost in Love.' It's doing well back home and it's going to be our first U.S. single."

Mae sang the CliffsNotes version of her story to the chorus of their song, *lost my tooth in the river back there | look like a jack-o-lantern but really don't care.*

"You know, there's another thing bothering me about your act," Chad said.

"What?" Russell asked. By his face I could tell he had been subject to Chad's constructive criticism long before we arrived.

"When you're singing your love songs, it feels like the lyrics are aimed at each other. It's kind of uncomfortable."

"Not at all. We're only alternating verses and harmonizing on the chorus," Graham said.

"I believe you. I'm just saying it sounds, and looks, like you're into each other. And both of you have your top four buttons undone. It makes your audience a little uneasy."

"There are plenty of American bands with two guys harmonizing," Russell said. "How about Loggins and Messina?"

"They sang about Winnie the Pooh and how their mama don't dance," Chad said. "They weren't pouring their hearts out to each other."

"What about Hall and Oates?" Graham asked.

"Tall blond and shorty with dark curls?" Chad said. "Are you guys copying their act? They sing about individual women, like a rich girl, or someone named Sara who smiles. And not very well, in my opinion. They'll be homeless by the eighties."

Anne rewarded Chad's comments with an over-the-top hearty laugh and rested her hand on his shoulder; a show of intimacy both Mae and I caught.

"You guys friends with AC/DC?" Anne asked. "That Bon Scott rocks. He's got a long career ahead of him."

"More importantly," Chad said. "Have either of you gotten into Olivia Newton-John's daks?"

"Nice Aussie speak, Chad," Russell said. "Wouldn't mind getting in those grundies. No offense, ladies."

More and more ranch guests joined the campfire. Mae and I changed out of our river clothes into something warmer. Chad and I invited Anne and her to share our cabin again and forgo camping before we all hiked out tomorrow, and they acquiesced with zero resistance. Ringtails, small mammals that looked like the spawn of raccoons and housecats, circled the fire looking for handouts. Baker and Ponch stopped by: Baker warned everyone to store food off the ground in hanging bags; Ponch tried to recruit females back to his cabin to stomp to the new Donna Summer double album, *Bad Girls*. Mae frightened him off with a toothless leer. I kept anticipating Chad attempting to recreate the flatulence scene from *Blazing Saddles*. Not so coincidentally, Chad and Anne both got tuckered out at the exact same moment. As they got up to go to our cabin, Chad leaned towards me and whispered, *give us an hour*, then embodied Wolfman Jack and shrieked a loud howl at the moon.

"Can we talk a minute," I said, and pulled him away from the fire.

Mae intervened with Anne.

"What are you doing?" I asked him. "One drug-induced slip-up I understand. It's entirely wrong, but I understand. You can't do it again, though. You're getting married later this month, asshole."

"I know. I know. I shouldn't," he said. "We have so much in common, though, and she's so self-confident and comfortable in her Super Woman body. Considering the circumstances this is going to sound odd, but I respect her. And she saved my life! I can't shake the image of her muscles twitching and veins bulging as she held that boulder up. I've found my own Diana Prince. Plus, it's like we're on a different planet down here, so there's no way Suzy finds out."

"You're willing to take the risk?" I asked. "Are you having doubts about marrying Suzy?"

"Absolutely not," he said unconvincingly. "It's just that Suzy is always so good to me. At times, almost too good, considering I'm not doing much to earn it. Her selflessness is enough for me, but I often wonder if it's enough for her? And we met at a campus fraternity party. I suppose you could call it part of a master plan, but it's more like *The Dating Game* for horny kids *with* booze *and* pot. Half of our fraternity is engaged or close to it. Anne and I, on the other hand, randomly met in the Grand Canyon. That's a totally different script. Kevin, for the pleasure we achieved this afternoon, this last shag is worth the risk."

"Shit! You already fucked her again?" I asked.

"Correction, you can't fuck someone her size," he said. "*She* fucks *you*. And what did you expect when you left us alone all afternoon in the cabin?"

"Seriously, that was the only activity you could think of? Couldn't you have talked, or played a board game, or shotputted boulders into the creek or something? Anything besides cheating on your fiancée?"

"Calm down. It'll be okay. Stop worrying about me."

"Unfortunately, I can't. It comes with the territory. And I was thinking more of Suzy."

"Whatever, I'm heading in. You should take a shot at Mae. Anne said she thinks you're a fox."

"Really?" I asked like a seventh grader. Her opinion chronologically preceded our afternoon adventure.

"Besides your little swim, did you guys have fun?" Chad pried. "Anything happen?"

"We talked a lot. She's dealing with some serious personal stuff."

"Oh no."

"Oh no, what?"

"You brought up faith, didn't you?" he asked.

"You say that like it's a sin," I said. "It's a part of me. And I thought she'd find it helpful. What's the big deal?"

"I'm not saying there's anything wrong with it, but I've seen this backfire on you repeatedly. You need to remember the three things you're not supposed to discuss when picking up chicks: religion, politics, and the Great Pumpkin." Chad grinned as he delivered his punch line.

I smiled to acknowledge we could agree to disagree on both of our matters, and no more conversation was necessary.

Armed with his stereo sidekick, he headed back towards our nearby cabin, less than fifty yards from the campfire, and Anne left Mae and joined him. At the door, Chad impressively, and precariously, swept Anne up, cradled her in his arms, and carried her sideways across the threshold.

"Well, I don't agree with it, but Anne thinks there's something special going on," Mae said. "Who am I to get in the way of the universe? Plus, would you try to stop something that big in heat?"

Aside from the crackling of the fire, hushed conversations, and chords Graham and Russell were experimenting with, Phantom

Ranch was totally silent. Mae stared into the fire; her mind was focused somewhere else. I stared into the fire; my mind was on her.

"He visited me during spring break this year," she said softly so only I could hear.

"Who?" I asked.

"My brother, Jamie. He was living at home with my mom in Phoenix, taking a couple of classes at a community college."

"Was he trying to get into a better school?"

"Not really. He was trying to stay out of trouble. School was never his thing. Anyway, we saw the *Buck Rogers* movie the first night he was in Tucson." She continued to stare into the fire.

"What did you think?" I asked.

"Thought it was square."

"Me too. Although, I think they're turning it into a TV series."

"After, we went over to my friend's house to play drinking games. Jamie was a hit with everybody from the start. One of my girlfriends was even digging on him. It started out as one of those times where I forgot all of the *other* times. Later, when using the bathroom, he tried to drink some water out of the sink. My brother had a rather large head and, I never knew this was possible, but, he ended up getting his head stuck. A guy had to go get tools and take the faucet apart."

"Was he okay?"

"Yeah. Throughout the ordeal he handled himself well. A few people laughed and he didn't take it personally like he usually does. When he was freed he even shared in the laugh. I was proud of him. But..."

"What?"

"We were playing quarters and one guy kept calling Jamie *sink boy. Drink sink boy, drink sink boy, drink sink boy.* It was in good fun, not a malicious tone whatsoever." Mae's voice cracked.

"What happened?"

"I could see Jamie's face transforming, as it had countless times before. He was never good with social cues. His mind turned him into a victim, and vilified everyone, including me. He threw his beer in the guy's face and invited him outside. Although large headed, my brother's short like me and would have gotten his ass kicked by this bigger guy. I intervened and, after calming him down enough to leave, took him back to my place. While I was making up the couch for him, I heard the hasty reverse and peel out of his Scirocco's tires."

"Where did he go?"

"He drove the two hours home in the middle of the night. He didn't say goodbye or anything. He was supposed to stay a week. Left a backpack full of clothes and a toothbrush."

"Did you make up?"

Mae wiped away slow rolling tears capturing the firelight. "He called a few days later. He always owned up to his outbursts and apologized for being disrespectful, rude, or whatever the case may be. He gave his usual speech about working on becoming a better person, and not such a screwup. His low self-esteem oozed through the phone. I felt so sorry for him. He didn't face challenges *in* his life. Life *was* his challenge. He could never get truly comfortable."

"Did he come back down for the rest of spring break?"

She did not answer. Her tears stopped.

"Mae?" I asked.

"I never saw him again," she said.

I put my right hand on top of her left and squeezed. It was the gesture of an old married couple, though it was instinctual. She deeply inhaled and exhaled, attempting to stave off floodwaters. Her gaze never left the center of the fire. We stayed like that for a few minutes.

Disturbing the silence, slicing through the night air with crystal clarity from the direction of our cabin, we heard a Wolfman-like voice say, "Close your eyes. I want to ride the skies in my sweet dreams."

"Was that Chad?" Mae asked.

I was grinning large at my friend's slightly too loud, and perfectly timed pillow talk and comic relief. "I think it was."

"Close your eyes. I want to see you tonight in my sweet dreams," Anne, equally audible and tacky, answered Chad.

Mae and I, along with the other fire patrons, did our best to hold back laughter and remain quiet in case there was more. Oddly, both members of Air Supply pulled out little notebooks and wrote in them.

"I wish I could carry your smile in my heart," Chad added. "For times when my life seems so low."

Anne answered, "It would make me believe what tomorrow could bring. When today doesn't really know."

This was too much. A few people lost it. Air Supply were writing furiously. Mae and I gaped at each other, anxious for more.

Chad obliged, "Anne, you're every woman in the world to me. You're my fantasy. You're my reality."

Anne responded, "You're everything I need. You're everything to me."

Mae resumed crying, this time from humorous pain. I joined her. Air Supply's pencils were getting a workout. Was this really happening? It was as if Jane Curtin and Bill Murray were taping a *Saturday Night Live* sketch, but these performances were not intentional comedy, or meant for an audience.

Anne chimed in again, "I know just where to touch you. And I know just what to prove."

Chad countered, "I know when to pull you closer. And I know when to let you loose."

Mae's conscience got the best of her. She gave a loud warning before censors were needed, "Anne, Chad, we can hear every word of your poetic foreplay and, although it's giving Air Supply new material, you might want to shut the fuck up and move on to the next step."

Lying in my bunk later, I did not want to let sleep abduct me into a new day—one with *no* guarantees. I stared up at the bottom of the top bunk, picturing the outline of Mae's body, which lay above. We had already consummated our relationship again, quietly enough to not wake Anne or Chad in the bunks next to us, but intensely enough for Mae to generate sufficient glow to protect a nighttime road crew.

I felt so unbelievably alive. I wanted time to stop so these feelings couldn't fade. I had stood on my pulpit many times and told others I was happy I was not going through life alone. I was always referring to God's presence, though. What I felt now, His presence and Mae's presence together, brought me to a whole new level of self-realization.

Was she staring up at the exposed rafters and contemplating where a path with me would lead? Or could this possibly have been just another inter-university, spring break–like, *zipless fuck* to her? Was I naive and ridiculous to believe anything different? While replaying today's home movie in my head, soundtracked by the Eagles' "Take It to the Limit," *all alone at the end of the evening | and the bright lights have faded to blue | I was thinking 'bout a woman who might have loved me | and I never knew,* sleep finally stole me.

In the dead of the night, I awoke to a flashlight shining in my face and someone whispering my name. Though I hoped it was Mae, it took me a few seconds to realize it was Chad, fully dressed and accessorized with pack, headband, and stereo.

"Time to escape," he whispered.

22. '01

The brownish-gray herd of mule deer, a dozen strong, was wide-eyed with a temporal lack of motor reactions. Mae slammed on the brakes, which made matters worse by accelerating us into a violent, out of control ice-spin. I had foolishly not been belted. I did not know if Mae was. Instinctively, I cocooned her body with mine, bracing for the imminent impact with deer, another car, tree, or anything else in the path of our Steel Curtain. The torque tried to pull me off, but I was pinned between her and the steering wheel, a fact I realized might not bode well for me. Nick Drake sang on, too focused on his own issues.

I was wearing my invisible backpack again, and although we were spinning sideways, I distinctly felt like I was falling, ass over teakettle. I hoped Mae's perpetual *Jaws* screen test–worthy scream would awaken the deer from their headlight hypnosis before the three-and-a-half-ton Cutlass did. We did more blind spins than the gal in *Ice Castles*. Even as the rotations slowed, I remained draped across Mae, ready for the worst. We eventually came to a stop in the middle of the road, facing toward the way we came, at the herd now stotting back into the forest. Somehow, we had miraculously avoided all of the blood and guts–filled bowling pins. A few stopped to look back at us, their source of potential danger. If they had middle digits in their cloven hooves I'm sure they would have flipped them.

Mae, who it turned out had been belted, was extremely shaken and apologizing profusely. Even after I repeatedly told her it was okay and we were okay, the *sorrys* kept flooding out. I thought she might be in shock. We switched places—I had sweated out every ounce of Miller Lite. Mae stopped apologizing and became quiet.

"Thank you," she eventually said.

I stared ahead, smiling and musing at what just happened. "You're welcome."

"No!" she said, and used her hand to firmly turn my head towards her so our eyes locked. "I'm thanking you for my life. You saved me." Her expression and manner of delivery woke me to the significance and gravity of the situation and her words. It was a familiar moment, and I felt her words encompassed much more than this incident. Her eyes washed over, triggering mine to follow.

I protectively wrapped my arms around her and held tight. I felt responsible for her. That always felt good. I knew she appreciated it, too. Our tears were interrupted by short, spontaneous giggles, then the joy of surviving yet another near tragedy in this blessed and cursed place overwhelmed us and we laughed uncontrollably the whole drive back to the El Tovar.

We hurried through the lobby, thankfully Pinto-less, and took the stairs, two at a time, up to the third floor. As we entered our room, our slate was wiped clean, our relationship was baptized, and most of our clothes, and all of Mae's hang-ups, were off before we even got the door shut behind us. Our striptease was infused with laughter as I quoted an inside joke, *I wish I could carry your smile in my heart, for times when my life seems so low,* and she responded, *It would make me believe what tomorrow could bring, when today doesn't really know.*

We discovered each other's bodies all over again and the sex felt both raw and meaningful, like our first few times, complete with Mae throwing the word *fuck* around with abandon like she was prone to in her youth. We satisfied a long-dormant hunger and ordered a gluttonous amount of room service, showered together, brought back encore sex from extinction, and fell asleep early in each other's arms.

When the morning light filtered through the drawn curtains, my eyes discerned a slight lightening of the blue carpet, from the color of Mae's old Calvin cutoffs to Twister circle. Wholly expecting to finally see the geological namesake of this place, I rolled out of bed and parted the curtains. The reward was a shade of gray infinitesimally softer than the last two days, but still thick enough to make the premium we spent for a view room seem like a scam.

I was alone at the window. Without the need to turn around and confirm, I knew the bed would be empty. I glanced about the room and acknowledged with my eyes what my heart and mind had already sensed; Mae was not there.

DAY 3

23. '01

Something was written on the nightstand notepad. My legs froze, unable to take the necessary steps to discover the words. I did not see her purse or car keys anywhere. I finally knew how her friend Anne felt twenty-two years ago when she awoke to my friend Chad's desertion—shock and denial.

I staggered over to the notepad, expecting to digest words more impactful and painful than a blind pinball collision with three-hundred-pound antlered animals, brain damage from underwater oxygen-deprivation, or the splintering of a skeleton after plummeting hundreds of feet onto solid rock. My mind saw *bye*, then *sorry*, before the light reflected off of it and instead revealed *walk* to my cornea. I was flooded with relief. I did not know why I was torturing myself like this since all signs from last night pointed to success. I scoured the room and found her purse and keys in the closet—confirmation the note was not a decoy.

I owed a call to my best friend since childhood, Chad. He was well aware of the current state of our marriage and the significance and potential consequences of this weekend. I knew he would be up at eight on a Sunday because of their two little ones. They had two older kids close in age to Warren and Hazel, but a few years ago his wife intimidated him into reversing his vasectomy, and then the house dealt them a pair; they should have named their twin boys *Mixed* and *Feelings*. At the time, I broached the possibility with Mae, thinking a baby might breathe new life into our relationship. She said the mere suggestion made her wonder if I knew her at all. She always resented my pressuring her into having kids so early in our marriage.

Chad picked up on the first ring. After we greeted each other, he commented, "Kevin, you wouldn't believe the size of these kids at one-and-a-half. I feel like I'm a Lilliputian raising baby Gullivers. So, the weekend's not going well?"

"Why would you think that?" I asked.

"I'm not supposed to tell you this, but Mae's called my other half a few times this weekend." Mae and she were close.

"And?" I asked.

"And it doesn't sound good."

"She's probably being dramatic," I said. "I think Mae feels it's fixable. And we had a *great* night last night. We put Farrah and Lee to shame."

"Buddy, that all sounds nice, but trust me, you need to change strategies, and you need to do it immediately."

I had to swallow my pride and admit I was too far inside my marriage to understand what it looked like from the outside. And over the years Chad had found his voice of reason, which I held for safekeeping in our youth. I seemed to have misplaced mine. "Why?" I asked.

"For years, through all of your marital challenges, I've tried to be supportive without hurting your feelings," he said. "But I've done you a grave disservice. Considering this is your last chance, I'm going to cut to the heart of it and be brutally honest."

"Please," I said.

"She's lived *your* life," he said.

"You mean *our* life."

"No. Listen to me. *Your* life and *her* life weren't fully compatible, so she's lived *your* life. If she had never met you, *her* life would be completely different."

"What's your point?" I asked. "If I never met her, *my* life would be different, too."

"How so? What dreams did you give up on?"

I stared intensely at the Indian blanket, then the blue carpet, and then the gray outside, expecting visions to appear like rapid fire. No *would'ves*, *should'ves*, or *could'ves* were eagerly waiting to be recalled. *My* life had met *my* expectations.

"Okay. Maybe it wouldn't," I admitted. "But Mae's not always like this. She's been extremely happy at times."

"She absolutely has," Chad said. "You've given her a lot to be happy about. Maybe more in the earlier years, but, nonetheless, a lot. And her ideology has conformed as much as possible to her environment. Frankly, if you hadn't changed so much, you might have pulled it off. Only…"

"Only what? And how do you think I've changed?"

"Only it's not something she can do forever. With the kids out of the house, she has an insatiable need to start living *her* life. And as for how you've changed, buddy; you're my best friend and I think you're great, but you didn't become the person I thought, and probably Mae thought, you'd become. Until you met Mae, you were on a path to get canonized. After you won her over, you took your foot off the gas a bit. You're simply more independent than you used to be."

"Better than anxious and insecure, right?" I said.

"Not necessarily. Is it better to seek answers, or feel like you already know them?"

I pondered the truths of his observation.

"I can help her," I said. "I can adjust and make *her* life more fulfilling." I was pacing back and forth, the length of the phone cord, with anxious energy.

"Kevin, I'm sure your intentions are good, but she has twenty-two years of empty promises and critical evidence working against you."

"So, what do you recommend I do?"

"You need to...hold on a second," he said, and covered the receiver.

"Jimmy, put down our Girlschool tape," Chad's muffled voice said.

His wife's voice in the background corrected him, "That one's Björn."

"How can you tell?"

"He's wearing your headband."

"Oh, yeah. Björn, give Daddy the tape."

I heard a small skirmish and then Chad returned. "Sorry. Where were we?"

"You were going to tell me what to do," I said.

"Right. Your only chance is to do something unexpected and out of character—something with an immediate impact. Good intentions are fucking worthless at this point."

"I had something planned for today," I said.

"Is it something that would shock her?"

"I don't necessarily think it would shock her, but I think she'll appreciate it."

"Do something different; bolder."

"But you don't even know what it is."

"It doesn't matter. It's your previous thinking, or lack thereof, that got you to this point. Do something different!"

My head spun. I looked at the bedside clock and could hear the hurried second-hand ticks. It was a déjà vu moment. My life had become a temperamental bomb ready to detonate any second, and I needed to remember which random wire to cut.

"I've got to go," Chad said. "Jimmy's trying to eat the *Perfection* pieces."

"Wait, do you have any suggestions?"

"I think you know what I suggest."

He and I had been down this path before.

"Use the force?" I asked.

"And when that fails, pray on it," he said. "Bye, Kevin."

I hollowed out as the wind left me, and sat down to support my emptiness. I was shocked by how oblivious I had become to such an obvious answer. I could not even remember the last time I sought His wisdom on how to live my life, or, more importantly, *our* life. I had gotten so used to driving without asking for directions, without even asking the hostage next to me where she wanted to go, getting more and more lost without knowing it. Twenty-two years ago, I told Mae her life would fill back up with meaningful stuff that would allow her to reflect on the loss of her brother from a positive place. Ironically, I had spent our twenty-two years together leaking meaningful stuff, and not refilling. At what point had I abridged unconditional love and support to a simple crutch I thought I could live without?

I dropped my head, closed my eyes, and apologized profusely for how I had strayed. How I had broken a promise to my wife about the man I would be. How I had been selfish instead of selfless, and my satisfaction blinded me to her dissatisfaction. How I had ended my intimate relationship with the teacher I was supposed to model my love after, lost my identity, and set myself, and our marriage, up for failure.

I prayed for forgiveness, the knowledge to fix myself, and more importantly, our marriage. I prayed for insight into what Chad referred to as *unexpected*, but would more appropriately be termed a *miracle*. I knew if I had His help I could save this, and it had been proven in this world that anything is possible. *God, grant me the serenity to accept the things I cannot change, the courage to change the things I can, and the wisdom to know the difference.*

I opened my eyes, and a huge pressure was lifted off my shoulders. How long had I been wearing the invisible backpack without realizing it? I walked back to the window and saw Tom the bartender shoveling snow away from an exterior storage closet. It set my mind in frantic motion. I grabbed emergency cash out of our suitcase, threw on my jeans and sweatshirt, and shot down the stairs and out the back door.

24. '79

"What time is it?" I whispered back to Chad.
"Four."

"Four? What are you thinking? Go back to bed." We had discussed leaving right after sunrise, while it was still cool out. There was definitely no mention of four. Neither Anne nor Mae stirred.

"Come outside," he said.

I crawled out of the bottom bunk in my t-shirt and boxers and followed him quietly across the cold cement floor. The acute pain from multiple bruises overrode the stiffness in my legs. Gently closing the front door behind us, I was chilled by the seventy-degree night air, having acclimated to the daytime triple digits. Not a sound could be heard in Phantom.

"I have to get out of here before she wakes up," he said.

"Oh, shit! Now your conscience kicks in."

"Kevin, this is my life I'm messing with here; mine and Suzy's life. I guess I needed to get this out of my system."

"You said you respected Anne because of her self-confidence."

He shrugged his shoulders. "Whatever. I wanted to get laid and justified it."

"I can't leave them."

"Why? You got what you wanted, too. Nice technique, by the way." He grinned.

I shook my head in disapproval of his voyeurism.

"So grab your pack and let's head out," he said.

"I think there's more than sex here," I said.

"More? There isn't any *more*. They live in Arizona and are going home today. I can assure you they don't want *more*. Didn't you notice they don't have a tent or sleeping bags on their packs? They came down here looking to shack up. If it wasn't with us it would have been with some other dudes."

Chad's observation and presumption critically wounded me.

"Plus," he said. "If you stay, you're going to shoulder the blame of my leaving."

He was right. Even if I did have a chance with Mae, this might destroy it.

"Couldn't we all hike out together, and then you can be an asshole later?" I pleaded.

"Do you realize what you are asking me to do? You want me to further risk my upcoming marriage to help you with your weekend fling? Seriously? Let's get out of Dodge."

"I'm staying," I said with uncertainty, because I now harbored doubts whether my presence would even be appreciated. And Chad was right about my selfish motives. Suzy would have been furious if I, who was supposed to be his voice of reason, foiled his escape.

"Wow. You really like this one." Chad tightened his shoulder and waist straps. "Well, I'm bummed to spend the day alone, but it makes me feel better knowing you're here for them. You can give them one of your little pep talks from the spirit in the sky. Once they're gone, meet me at the El Tovar and we can get a good dinner and hit the lounge tonight before we drive back to S.D. tomorrow. May the force be with you." He smirked stupidly.

"And also with you," I obliged as we shook hands.

He lit his path and headed out of Phantom towards the Colorado. The door creaked open behind me and Mae stuck her head out.

"What are you doing?" she whispered.

"Chad left," I said.

"What? Shit! Poor Anne. Fucking asshole." She came out in her t-shirt and underwear and stood next to me, looking out to see if Chad was catchable. He had disappeared into the night.

"Can I help you two with something?" someone asked us. Mae shrieked and, embarrassingly, I shrieked louder. Standing no more than three feet to the side of us on the porch was Ranger Carroll, dressed in his ranger hat, white undershirt, boxers, and dark socks with no shoes. He seemed oblivious to the fact we were all standing there in our underwear. Mae's hands were in front of her crotch.

"Just saying goodbye to a friend hiking out on Bright Angel," I said.

"Were they hiking alone? Male or female?" he asked me.

"Yes. Male."

"I'll call up to Indian Garden and tell them to be on the lookout for him," he said.

"Thank you."

"I'm going to finish my rounds now. You two have a nice day."

Mae and I exchanged puzzled looks as Ranger Carroll headed out on his repetitive loop. We heard hurried footsteps approaching and saw the ranger's wife, in a nightgown, stop her husband, whisper something in his ear, and push him in the direction of their cabin, which he walked to without any further discussion. She saw us and came over.

"Did he wake you?" she asked.

"No. We were out here talking and he surprised us," I said.

"I'm sorry," she said. "He snuck out of bed."

"Does he always do rounds this early?" Mae asked.

"It's unpredictable, but sometimes," she said.

"Is he...okay?" Mae asked.

"Unfortunately, no. He's in the later stages of dementia," she said.

"I'm so sorry," Mae said. "It's impressive he can still be a ranger."

"That's kind of you," she said, "but he hasn't been a ranger in nearly twenty-five years. Neither of us has been."

"What do you mean?" I asked.

"We were both rangers here at Phantom Ranch until 1955, when we wanted to start a family and John took a teaching position at the University in Flagstaff."

"But the uniform, and his rounds, and all of the advice he gives?" I asked.

"I know. It's a bit confusing," she said. "Earlier this year, when his condition was advancing at an alarming rate, I took him here to say goodbye. Phantom Ranch always held a special place in his heart: the blending of these rustic buildings into the magnificent rock backdrop; the constant stream of guests who came here *not* to get away from it all, but to find it all; and, most importantly, our love story was down here."

"And how did it go?" I asked.

"The most unexpected and miraculous thing happened when we arrived," she said. "Blocks of his memories I had written off as lost came streaming back, including almost everything from our Phantom Ranch years. I realized the Grand Canyon is part of us and he's at his best when we're all together. So, I got permission from the National Park Service to rent out a cabin down here for six months, and as long as I follow him around and make sure he does not give out any dangerous advice, they're fine with the arrangement. And that ratty old uniform is from 1955, but don't tell him. I keep it cleaned and pressed as much as possible, but it's falling apart."

"You fell in love down here?" Mae asked.

"John was turned down by the Army in World War II because of an irregular heartbeat," she said. "His inability to defend his country tormented him, so he became a National Park ranger to defend the monuments that define our country. He had been posted in Phantom Ranch for two years before I was assigned here in 1945. We fell madly in love and felt like the two luckiest people in the world to be able to wake up here together every day." Jeanne spoke in hushed tones, but the story was loud in emotion and awe.

"What about the spot in front of the employee bunkhouse he stops at when he's doing his rounds, and the dancing on the picnic table?" Mae asked.

She smiled. "That's where the swimming pool used to be. Confuses him every darn time. And it was while dancing on the picnic table we first expressed our love for each other. Also, it's where he proposed."

"I envy you," I said.

"Why?" she asked, surprised.

"You have a remarkable story to tell," I said. "I know it's not ending how you planned, but you found a way for both of you to fall in love all over again."

Jeanne cried silent tears of joy. "This was a way for me to honor how amazing of a man he was. But, you're right, at times it feels like we're back in 1945 and I am overcome by the intensity of our young love. Even after he's gone, I'll find a job at the canyon, any job, taking pictures of tourists on mules, greeting people at the visitor center, working at the village post office, whatever. I want to stay in the place where his heart and, therefore, my heart, are at their strongest."

Mae hung on every word and glowed an early sunrise.

"I better go and make sure John got back okay," Jeanne said. "Nice chatting with both of you. Thank you." As she walked away she stopped and turned back to us. "Did you two meet here?"

"Yes," I said.

"Why?" Mae asked.

"No reason," she said, and smiled. "I could just tell."

25. '01

After overcoming each of Tom's objections by steadily increasing the size of the stack of cash in his palm, I got him to agree to help me with the plan I had concocted in less than five minutes. I continued out to the rim trail and jogged west to where I was sure Mae would be. I moved much more swiftly without the invisible backpack. It was considerably warmer than yesterday, and the snow had melted off the trail. It would be unwise to stray anywhere off the right side of the trail because the snow cover still hid the adjacent canyon's edge. A sea of chipmunks, looking for handouts, parted as I passed. Visibility was a little better today, hopeful instead of yesterday's despondent, but the canyon remained in hiding.

I thought unceasingly about my course of action—seemingly perfect at creation, but now slowly filling me with dread. After passing the other lodges and then the Bright Angel trailhead, I spotted Mae in the distance, gazing into the Bright Angel Fault from the Trailview Overlook along Hermit Road. I was sure she was trying again to see, and hopefully feel, our past.

As I slowed to a walk and then timidly neared her from behind, I witnessed a resonant, heartwarming sight. The outline around Mae and her golden U of A fleece and jeans was surrounded by bright, warm, fuzzy edges. Her long-lost glow had triumphantly returned when I least expected it. Chad was absolutely, negligently, indisputably wrong. I had assumed the worst from a bad tip and formulated an asinine, unnecessary game plan. Her radiance was the validation, I sought, that last night meant something to her also. I knew you could not fake that level of intensity, and for her, like me, it must have felt like the first time again—a new beginning. Mae's inner light had always shone the brightest when her soul affirmed her choices and feelings.

The glow had dimmed over the years. While I caught an occasional glimpse during precious moments with the kids, or in photographs from her mission trips, it was not something I had been a catalyst for anymore. I had longed, more so than for any other object or result in my life, to see this shine again, to be the switch, the stimulus, the cause, the reason for why she felt in perfect alignment with her destiny. *Long as I can see the light*, Creedence sang, prior to breaking up.

The trail made a slight turn, and the direction I approached from shifted from west to south. Her glowing outline vanished instantly; it had been a cruel illusion caused by the angle of the morning sun, hidden sheepishly in the fog. The possibility of happiness, without change, had been an illusion, more so than the hidden canyon. My head and heart recognized the lack of options at a dead-end. Since the glow was also absent during last night's sex, and I was convinced she did not fake her intensity, instead of feeling like the first time again for her, it must have felt like the only other occurrence able to reach those levels—the last. Shifting gravel under one of my shoes announced my presence, and Mae's head turned slightly, revealing a stream of tears through the field of freckles on her rounded cheek.

"If you're planning on jumping," I said. "Remember to shout an overused phrase first."

"Please don't squeeze the Charmin," she said, and struggled to smile, as her fair skin turned towards me. She made a valiant effort to impact her dimples, but the moment her espresso eyes connected with mine, they drowned before hiding behind a thick veil of lashes. The silence that followed said everything. It was too late for *the* talk.

"Mae, I know," I said. "You want something different."

She opened her eyes. "Kevin, I'm so sorry."

My face felt like a wet sponge receiving pressure from behind.

"It's something I have to do," she continued. Words and sobs alternated. "It's probably insane to walk away from a safe, comfortable life with you. I know how our church feels about it; I'm the villain here. You never committed any sin that threatened the sanctity of our marriage."

"That's not true," I said.

"It's not?" she asked, disoriented. Her curiosity blocked her tear ducts.

"My path has been littered with broken promises, selfish acts, and lip-service faith. Can you honestly say we'd be at this impasse today if I had remained the man I promised I would be, if I had welcomed our challenges instead of avoiding and ignoring them, if I had prioritized my relationship with you over the children, if I had remembered I was born with two ears and only one mouth and used them in the ratio intended, if I had sought yours and prayerful wisdom on every important family decision, if I had remembered that our differences brought us together in the first place and they should have been encouraged instead of neutralized?"

"Not necessarily. Maybe. Probably. Truthfully, I don't know," she said.

I knew, though. It was primarily my fault we were here, right back where we started, at the Bright Angel Fault. I had taken so many wrong turns that this had been our only hope of finding our way. And it worked. At least it did for Mae. The chipmunks, noticing our stationary discussion, had crept closer and closer, as if I would whip out a Marathon bar at any moment. I had an overwhelming desire to punt one of them into the canyon.

"Don't you wish I had done a better job at all of those things?" I asked.

"Of course I do. Don't you?" Her tears remained at bay.

"More than anything. I truly wish I would have changed more for you. I still think I can."

"It's ironic, Kevin. Even though I knew we had our differences when we met, I think I would have been fine if you never changed at all. I never needed you to be more like me. I needed you to be more like you. You can't turn back time, though."

I was flipping over the railing again, and this time she wasn't going to save me.

"We just weren't meant to be *forever*," she said.

My eyes dampened.

She continued, "You're a good father and provider, and together we raised two well-adjusted beautiful young adults—not an easy task. And you're responsible for introducing me to Christ, a relationship that made my life infinitely more meaningful. I'm fully convinced He sent you to me, as His disciple, after my brother died. I was vulnerable and would have been easy prey for darker influences. You taught me to seek hope in a time of despair. You've always made me feel safe, no matter what, and that's the scariest thing for me to leave behind. And we have so many memories I cherish and would never change. Do you remember how hard you tried, no matter how uncomfortable, to be outgoing and adventurous with me when we were young? I loved it. Kevin, you are one horrible singer, but I loved every word you ever sang. I love you, Kevin. I'll always love you. We had a good life together."

Had broke my dam.

She went on, "And I don't think it was a mistake marrying you. I was meant to marry you. It's just, I don't feel like I'm living *my* life anymore within our marriage, and I need to live *my* life."

Even though it sounded like a tribute, it *only* felt like failure. It reminded me of the speeches I heard in AYSO soccer before being handed my participation trophy. I was being dumped by my wife; I was being dumped by the mother of my children; I was being dumped by my partner, my companion, my mate, my *lover*. One of the chipmunks entered the launch area. It took every ounce of restraint to resist.

"I thought we came here to talk about our issues," I pleaded.

"I did, too," she said. "But by you continuing to avoid them, it's given me plenty of time to think. And I've gotten to the point where I'm at peace with my decision."

If I had not been so ignorant to her making decisions in the first place, she never would have made this one. I wanted to make all of this go away. I wanted to start over. I wanted to rewind to the day we met.

"Mae, I understand you're at peace with your decision, but I need you to be adventurous with me one last time. I need you to have blind faith that I *do* have the ability to change, to change *back*, and I need you to go with me someplace right now where I can prove it." Nothing can stop the man with the right mental attitude from achieving his goal.

"Kevin, it's too late. I've made up my..."

I interrupted her. I had to. I was not going to let the success story about why two very different individuals felt compelled to spend their lives together after just three days get unwritten. If the right attitude was restorable, so was the goal. "Mae, I swear to God, right after I recited the serenity prayer, this was His answer."

Mae looked like a mule deer in the headlights. From her pro-longed cliffhanger silence, I did not know whether she left her fate open to one last temptation.

"Okay," she said. "I'll go with you."

26. '79

It was difficult falling back asleep after Chad's early departure and our run-in with the Carrolls. Based on the shifts and creaks bombing from her bunk, Mae was experiencing a similar challenge. When I reopened my eyes for the second time in the young day, it was because an open window let in a much needed breeze, and morning light that spotlighted our weekend's sheddings on the cement floor: crumbs, beer cans, long strands of hair, and a couple of ripped-open square wrappers under Chad and Anne's bunks.

Anne, in her gray U of A tank and cutoffs, was already up getting her pack ready. Mae was in the bathroom.

"What time is it?" I asked Anne.

"Six-thirty."

"Oh, crap. We better get going," I said. *We* felt like an assumptive pronoun.

"Yep. Try to at least beat some of the heat. Packing extra water this time," she said.

I scanned her pack. Chad was right: no tent, no sleeping bag. I glanced at Mae's resting against the wall—same. This bothered me, but I corked any questions.

"How soon can you be ready?" she asked.

"Twenty minutes."

"Okay, but don't lag. I'll go to the canteen and grab us muffins and bananas and turn in your cabin key. You want coffee?"

"Please."

Anne must have discovered four minus one equaled three by now, but there was no sign of anger or disappointment in her voice.

"You two behave," she said, and exited.

Mae came out of the bathroom wearing her day one outfit: hair pulled back by a mustard headband, white embroidered peasant top, cutoff jeans, and hiking boots.

"Anne's not pissed?" I asked.

"She's in denial," Mae said. "When she woke up she was in shock, so I guess she's progressing."

"How are you?"

"A little tired, but okay. This was quite the unexpected weekend."

"Good unexpected?" I ventured.

"Except for the flirtations with death."

I had hoped I would be cited specifically in her answer.

"Agreed," I said. "What are you doing the rest of the summer? Traveling?"

"I wish. I'll see the world after graduation. My mom needs me at home this summer because of Jamie. My dad's remarried and lives nearby, so I'll see him some, too. I'm taking a couple of extra classes at a local junior college and waitressing at a fried chicken and waffle restaurant my friend's parents own. Probably start my senior year twenty pounds heavier. Anne's from Phoenix, too, so she'll be training there all summer." She paused in thought.

"Having a brother who committed suicide makes me a bit of an outcast now," she continued. "Most people try to steer clear of me because they don't know how to act or what to say. Anne and I can relate more now. We've both been shipwrecked on the island of misfit toys. She's a really loyal person and friend, and I need that now. When do you start working for your uncle?"

"After Chad's wedding at the end of the month."

"Looking forward to it?"

"It's a place-keeper."

"Yeah. You've said that. Until something more *meaningful*, right?"

I noticed she inflected hope, not disappointment, this time.

"Right."

The new day, likely our last together, had diluted our intimacy, and our conversational rhythm was slightly off. Either Mae's force field that I had successfully disarmed yesterday was back up, or I was overthinking my first few waking minutes. To be in wardrobe sync with them, I recycled my *I'm a Pepper* t-shirt.

Anne returned and proclaimed, "You ready? I want to *get the fuck* out of here as soon as we can."

Oh joy, an angry hike.

A steady stream of hikers began leaving Phantom Ranch and the Bright Angel Campgrounds, most heading back up to the south rim, with few heading in the opposite direction on the North Kaibab trail towards the north rim. Anne led us at a torrid pace, and I wondered whether we were hiking or hunting. Conversation beyond small talk was a challenge due to overburdened lungs and a constant focus on not falling behind.

In the middle of the Silver Suspension Bridge, without breaking pace, Anne's volcano began erupting, "You know your friend fucked with my head."

"Excuse me?" I asked.

"He kept saying he felt a deep connection to me, and it was making him reevaluate his engagement."

"Whatever it took to get into your cutoffs," Mae added fuel to the fire.

"I know that now, but it felt different," Anne said, and picked up her pace, which I did not think was humanly possible.

I wanted to say something to soothe her nerves, and therefore slacken her pace, without risk of getting thrown in the river. "Anne, since you knew he was engaged, didn't you assume it would just be a fling?"

"Yeah, at first," she said huffily. "We got along so damn well, though. Maybe it was because there was no pressure. I think we let our guards down—at least I did—and real feelings spilled out. It felt like we were a real couple during our brief time together." The longing to be part of a *real* couple could plainly be heard in her voice.

"But he's getting married in a few weeks," I said.

"I know. I know," she said, frustrated. "Then why would he keep saying how much he admired me? Not just how far I could throw a nine-pound metal ball, but *all* of me. He was already in my cutoffs at that point."

We were now trucking along the River trail, maintaining a speed that carried a high risk of rolling an ankle in the hidden pockets of deep sand.

"He probably said it because he meant it," I said. "Is it unheard of for a guy to have strong feelings for more than one girl, to admire and appreciate different traits, to discover something new they didn't know they were missing?" It took a high level of exertion to get intelligent thoughts out through my hard-pumping lungs.

She relaxed her pace. "I suppose not," she said.

"It's probably why he left without saying goodbye," I said, breathing a little easier. "He was into it deeper than he wanted to be and got conflicted and scared."

Satisfied with the explanation, Anne slowed to a normal pace and Mae and I, who had been trailing, practically ran her over. Mae had been a quiet observer but was now shaking her head and rolling her eyes disbelievingly.

"Why do you always do that?" Mae asked me accusatorially.

"Do what?" I asked.

"Try to make awful situations sound positive. It's as if Richard Dawson asked you to name the top ways to convince people shit doesn't stink."

"What do you mean?"

"You made my dead brother a pampered sparrow, told the ranger's wife her husband's dementia gave them an enviable life, and are trying to convince Anne that your good friend, who is fucking around behind his soon-to-be wife's back, did a noble thing by bailing and letting her pick up the condom wrappers. Why can't you keep your opinions to yourself and let people grieve without interruption? You're like a character in *Ordinary People* who wanted Conrad to act normal after all he went through, because it would make them feel more comfortable."

"Not at all," I said defensively. "What's wrong with trying to be helpful? Trying to provide hope in a time of despair?" I asked.

"Not every situation needs a savior, Kevin." Somehow, every ounce of Anne's anger had transferred to Mae, and was now aimed at me.

She continued, "Don't make guarantees. You said it yourself, the only guarantee we're given is that life won't be easy. Bad things happen to good people and that's all there is to it. Your friend screwed over my friend—fact! My brother took his life because he was depressed—fact! Why try to disguise them as anything else? Why do you have to look for a positive message, rainbow, or fucking silver lining? With your self-proclaimed clairvoyance, can you honestly say life is guaranteed to get better?"

I was at a loss for words. I tried to be supportive and it belligerently backfired. And she was not just attacking my words, but my character, and I felt I had a right to fight back. I was not going to cower and apologize for trying to pick someone up when they were down. It was my prerogative how I reacted to other people's troubles. And it was this line of single-minded, ignorant thinking that triggered the firing of the only bullet rattling around in my chamber: *if you two weren't planning on hooking up this weekend, then why didn't you bring your own tent or sleeping bags?* My conscience immediately flagged the error of my rash response.

Mae and Anne stopped dead in their deep sand tracks.

"Are you serious?" Mae asked. "Do you think we're a couple of whores who would've hooked up with anybody to get a free room? Have you been feeling like you got used?"

"No. Sorry. I was only curious," I said timidly.

"First of all," Mae said, "just because we're broke and were hoping to find a free place to stay does not mean we planned on using our bodies as payment. Second, even if we knew it was a possibility, we're adults in charge of our own bodies and we can do whatever we fucking please. I do *not* need to be judged by you." Mae resumed Anne's original pace.

I raced to catch up with her, but Anne held me back. "Let her release some angry energy," she said. "She needs to get it out."

We stayed in silent single-file formation, with Anne buffering Mae and me, as we left the Colorado and started our ascent. The temperature, which was already pushing eighty, would now stay relatively consistent because of the progression of the day being countered by the twenty-degree differential from bottom to top.

With the static of the river fading, Anne broke the long silence when we entered the steep Devil's Corkscrew switchbacks, "I didn't used to be this easy."

"What?" Mae asked.

"I'm what guys consider *easy*, but I wasn't always this way."

"Anne, you're not easy," Mae said.

"Mae, I *am*. I'll screw anything if they express interest in me." Her tone was far from proud.

"When I started dating back in high school," she continued, "my plan was to protect my virtue until guys got to know me better."

"Makes sense," Mae said.

"I thought so," Anne said. "Turns out, though, guys didn't want to get to know me better. Guys asked me out because I was a novelty, curiosity, or line item on a scavenger hunt. They wanted to be able to point at me and tell their friends they conquered me. They were too horrified to ever introduce me as their girlfriend. I got pathetically few second dates. So, I shifted gears."

The saddest part of Anne's remarks was the undeniable truth about male immaturity.

"What do you mean, shifted gears?" Mae asked.

"I eliminated the chase and let them catch me. I was hoping after they had sex with me they would want to come back for more, and then we could get to know each other better. Well, it didn't work like I thought it would. You know how many guys came back for seconds with *Any-man Annie?*"

"No," Mae said softly.

"Not one. Not one single sequel screw. What's ironic is even though I've had a lot of sex, it's never been great because feelings have never been involved. And yes, neither of you need to state the obvious. I've read enough psych class textbooks to understand they have no respect for me because I'm not exhibiting self-respect myself. I get it."

"What about Chad?" Mae asked. "He came back for more."

"I suppose," Anne said. "And it felt like we connected. Still, same end result as the others."

"Anne, he's getting married this month," Mae said.

"Yeah, you both keep reminding me. I guess a small part of me felt I could change that."

I opted to break my silence, "This is the moment when I would state something like *if you let the beautiful person inside of you shine as bright as possible, you'll be amazed at the genuine response.* But, I'm not going to because Mae will accuse me of adding a, how did you put it, Mae? Oh yeah, a *fucking silver lining.*"

"Whatever," Mae said, half-laughing, removing me from her shit list.

All morning we listened for Chad's homing device, the stereo, but heard nothing. Nor had we seen any identifiable specks on distant portions of the trail. We arrived at Indian Garden at ten-thirty. I overheard one of the rangers speaking on his walkie-talkie to a ranger back down at Phantom Ranch: *He came through here a couple hours ago, alone. Must have had a fight with his boyfriend. Are you sure you didn't see them down there this weekend?* I pretended my feet fascinated me as I hiked through.

Continuing up the Tonto Platform, the visual of the remaining sharp rise and elevation of the canyon walls made it appear an impossibility to hike out of. If we hadn't hiked down on this same Bright Angel trail, I would have assumed we took a wrong turn sometime today. Traffic picked up with day hikers, and we encountered our first mule train before climbing Jacob's Ladder.

Towards the top of the switchbacks, as a helicopter tour buzzed overhead down the Bright Angel Fault, Anne declared the revelation, "I'm not going to put out anymore unless a guy respects me."

"Good for you," Mae said with some exertion. Our lightning fast first leg was paying negative dividends.

"Yay," I said, to celebrate her celibacy. What was the appropriate response to the marking up of a previously free product?

I had spent most of the last few hours in quiet prayer and deep thought on more weighty topics than Anne's easiness: *Was it a naive, unrealistic, and mentally unhealthy belief that hope and despair could coexist? Was I putting too much emphasis on faith, with not enough empathy for suffering, since faith is often born out of suffering?* It was difficult to cleanly meditate on areas of personal growth when part of my mind stayed tethered to the idea of Mae: *was I a few miles away from never seeing her again, and was that reality as painful for her as it was for me?* Since the earlier confrontation, conversation had been light but there had been a symphony of stolen glances. All thoughts, questions, and feelings were streams feeding into my internal river of confusion: *what was my next move in the game of life?* With no answers revealed, all I could do was keep putting one boot in front of the other; hiking out of the security of adolescence into the abyss of adulthood.

We stopped for a much-needed shade break inside the three-mile resthouse. The remaining portion of our hike, the steepest, would be the most physically and mentally challenging. Freed from the burdens of our packs, I sat across from the girls and we reclined on the benches and snacked. The only other person in the resthouse was a guy sitting in the corner with a golden box of cereal in his lap. He was oblivious to us and apparently relished his cereal, based on the obnoxious sounds of joy accompanying his chewing. I recognized him. I had seen too many simply plotted, quickly scripted, badly acted, dumbed-down, unthought-provoking, but somehow amusing, live action Disney films to not recognize the *real* Kurt Russell. I motioned with my hand to Mae, who upon recognition motioned to Anne, who upon recognition pried free hair strands plastered to her face with sweat and salt. Her head reddened as she worked up the nerve to address her celebrity crush.

"Aren't you Kurt Russell?" Anne asked.

"I am," he said through a mouthful of cereal.

"I thought you were great as Elvis."

"Thank you. Thank you very much," he said in a cheesy Elvis impression.

Anne laughed heartily.

"Have any of you tried this new cereal?" Kurt asked us after he swallowed.

We all looked at his box of *Waffelos* featuring a cartoon cowboy with a large handlebar mustache, a cartoon horse playing a guitar, and what looked liked waffle squares falling into a bowl of milk, and shook our heads.

"It's far out," he said. "The squares taste like waffles with maple syrup mixed right in. I can't get enough of them." He was genuinely—disturbingly—excited about this cereal.

"Groovy," Anne said. "Can I try?"

Kurt looked down into his box. "Well, I'm almost out. You can buy a box at the village grocery store."

"Cool," Anne said with a hint of disappointment in her voice.

Kurt returned to stuffing his mouth with artificial waffle squares and was indifferent to our presence. It pained me to see this display of male insolence so soon after Anne declared her desire for respect. I could tell from her face, it pained Anne more.

"Let's get out of here," Mae suggested.

"Okay," Anne said dejectedly.

Anne, without her pack, was sitting on a cliff's edge near the resthouse when Mae and I came out of the bathrooms. Mae and I exchanged worried glances. To our relief, she stood up, faced us, and dusted the red off the back of her cutoffs. As she did so, a large piece of shale beneath her feet broke off and then slipped over the edge, taking her with it like a skimboard. Her eyes widened in shock as she fell in a backwards, stand-up position. She instinctively shot out her arms and dug her claws into the earth as deep as the parched soil would let her. Forearm, triceps, shoulder, and back muscles swelled to mythical proportions as they anchored her, from the breasts up, on the ledge, and the shale skimboard continued rider-less until it exploded on impact somewhere below.

A sense of relief crossed Anne's face when she stopped her fall, but it was only momentary as her left grip loosened, and her expression matched mine from the railing—the realization she was in a losing battle with physics. Mae and I ran towards her and yelled *Kurt* since he was the closest. Kurt Russell came out of the resthouse, Waffelos in hand, spotted Anne, and looked around in panic for someone else who might be able to help, wasting precious seconds since we were the only ones there.

Mae and I reached her first. Her entire body below her shoulders was now dangling over the edge. I peeked around her, hoping to see a ledge or gradual descent, but saw only nothingness. Both of her grips were earth-based and fragile and could break free any second. Mae sat and grabbed Anne's left arm while I sat and grabbed her right. It was hard to get any leverage with our feet so close to the edge. Her enlarged sweaty arms were difficult to get a tight grip on. I pulled with every ounce of energy in my body, stretching surf muscles to their limits and feeling like my head might explode. Mae was equally taut and some of her freckles popped out into the third dimension. Being mere mortals, unlike our victim, the three of us were slowly sliding, signaling the canyon was winning. I looked over my shoulder to see Kurt Russell, who had actually starred in *The Strongest Man in the World*, still running around frantically with his box of cereal in hand.

Anne's eyes were those of a little girl who lost her favorite stuffed animal and its security. She was fully aware what was happening as her fulcrum became uncorrectable. She kept her sliding grip on the ground, knowing if she grabbed us we would be pulled over with her. We were mere moments away from when Mae and I would mind-screwingly need to consciously let go of her. I could already hear the distinct crack from the pending impact of her body on the rock below. Mae was crying. Only Anne's forearms, pumped up and looking like a Popeye-lobster crossbreed, were left to make a futile last clinging effort.

Out of the side of my right eye, I saw Mae get pulled off of Anne's left arm, while someone else hurriedly wrapped something red, white, and blue around it.

27. '01

Mae headed upstairs to make a call, while I waited in the lobby before we drove to our destination. Sitting alone, I felt my anxiety level rise in anticipation. I saw Tom come out of the closed lounge, his jacket rolled up under one arm, and lock the door behind him. He did not notice me as he headed to the exit.

"Tom," I said, startling him. He dropped his jacket, and a bottle of whiskey rolled out of it.

"You scared me," he said.

My eyes were on the whiskey.

"Oh, this?" he said. "Management doesn't like me carrying inventory through the lobby because of the kids. Are we still on?"

"Yes," I said. "She'll be down soon and we'll meet you there."

"I'd better get a move on," he said, and rewrapped the bottle before exiting.

Mae came down a few minutes later.

"You make your call?" I asked.

"Yes, but I couldn't get a hold of them," she said.

"Was it important?"

"It'll be okay. So where are we going?"

"It's a surprise. Come on." I offered my arm and escorted her out to the car. She would refuse to go if I gave her any details. Looking in the direction of the canyon, visibility remained zero zero, but the hopeful softening trend continued.

The snow and ice had melted off the roads and the only ill driving effect was the thick brown crud frosting the lower half of the Cutlass. With increased purpose came increased speed. We followed yesterday's route, and as we headed out the park gates with the heavy Sunday exodus traffic, scarcer incoming park traffic was being welcomed by only one operating booth. In between greeting visitors, the Richard Dreyfuss lookalike was again outside working on his snow-based Devils Tower.

We drove past the turnoff to yesterday's wildlife viewing/thrill ride, and then through Tusayan and its motels, family restaurants, gas stations, and canyon novelty shops. My palms were sweating into the steering wheel. When we exited town Mae looked agitated because there was a whole lot of nothing up ahead. We were an hour from Williams, an hour-and-a-half from Flagstaff, and three-and-a-half hours from her family and our good friends in Phoenix. I could tell from her scrunched-up face that my last chance came with a concise time limit. She might have thought I was taking her to the nearest tourist attraction, Bedrock City. Less than a minute later, when we passed the north entrance to the Grand Canyon Airport, Mae let out a sigh of relief. When I turned on my right turn signal as we approached the south entrance to the airport, she choked on her sigh.

"No, Kevin. We're not doing this."

"We are," I said with a smirk.

"No. We can't. *You* can't."

"I *can*," I said, as I turned into the entrance, drove past the main terminal building, and pulled into the parking lot next to the helicopter facilities.

When I swiveled out of the Cutlass my legs were unsteady. My heart beat in double-time and I felt a collapsing pressure on my chest. Mae was far from empathetic of my choice to tackle this demon in the name of our marriage. She was pissed off and trying to dissuade me, clearly remembering previous stressful situations caused by this phobia. Seven freshly painted helicopters, fleets of four and three, were parked on the apron next to a helipad occupied with a more worn, older-looking, military-green model. It had a badly faded brown, red, orange, and yellow paint job on the side that looked like bacon and eggs in a frying pan. This was all eerily familiar.

We walked by the adjoining offices of three tour companies. The first two were closed and had signs in their windows saying tours would resume this afternoon *pending weather improvement.* The light was on in the third, and we opened the door to a room with four foldout chairs with deeply stained upholstered seats, and a disheveled office area. Two early Van Halen concert promotion posters, colors faded to grays, were pinned to one wall with thumbtacks: headlining at Gazzarri's and headlining at Whisky a Go Go. No one was there, so we sat and waited in the stained seats.

"Good news and good news," said Tom, when he came in five minutes later, rolled-up jacket under his arm. "The tower says the sun is shining on the north rim, so we're likely to see something this morning." He introduced himself to Mae.

"What's the other good news?" she asked.

"They reinstated my license," Tom said with a big grin.

"Why was it not *in*stated?" I asked.

"Misunderstanding."

"Which was?"

"I had an open bottle of Jack in my ride."

"Why?" I asked.

"It was after work. I was only cleaning."

"Then why did you get in trouble?"

"The battery was powered on. When the battery's on, you're technically flying. Like I said, a misunderstanding."

I was waiting for him to say *smile, you're on* Candid Camera.

"Do you have a bathroom here?" Mae asked.

"In the back of the building," Tom answered and pointed to the front door as her route.

As soon as Mae left Tom unrolled his jacket on the desk and pulled out the bottle of Jack from the lobby.

"Are you fucking kidding me?" I asked, jumping up.

"Relax! It's not for me, Kevin. Listen. I thought I recognized you at the bar but couldn't figure out why. This morning it dawned on me that you and your wife were my first passengers twenty-two years ago. Can you believe it? And I distinctly remember you freaked out back then. If you don't want any, that's cool."

I eyed the bottle, volume noticeably lower than in the lobby, and then the front door, and then the bottle again. It couldn't hurt. I nodded and he filled a Dixie cup. I smoothly downed the room temperature full-flavored whiskey in one gulp. He dangled the bottle in front of me again. I looked to the front door and gave him another nod. The rapid-fire second dose met a little resistance and burned my throat. He offered me a Ramblin' root beer to swig around and cover up the smell, and wrapped the bottle back up in his coat.

Mae returned and I overreacted, "Tom gave me a root beer."

"Okay," she said quizzically, not sure why this was newsworthy.

"I have to go grab something out of my car," Tom said. "Can you please sign these waivers?" He handed us two clipboards and walked out with his coat.

While I wondered why he didn't hide the bottle someplace in his office, warmth and a new attitude overtook me and masked all inhibitions.

"Are you actually *smiling*?" Mae asked.

Shit. I was sporting a buzz-smirk.

"Thinking positive thoughts," I said goofily.

"Let's hit it," Tom said, on his return.

We followed him out to the helipad where his whole fleet was parked, one Huey, which he said saw action in Vietnam. The faded paint job on the side, which he said he had done himself, was supposed to be a canyon vista at sunrise, but passengers collectively thought it looked more like someone cooking breakfast. Although our ex-military chariot was boxier, less streamlined, and had fewer exterior windows than the other more commercial–looking rides, it looked sturdier and tougher. As my flying phobia got out of hand over the years, I paid excruciatingly close attention to every flight detail: weather, equipment, staff, route, *bumps*.

As I climbed inside, the whiskey seemed to mysteriously vaporize from my system. I breathed deep and tried to deny my mind clear, sober thinking. Just enough of the mask remained to keep me from bolting in panic. I looked out at a limp windsock on a nearby flagpole and was thankful for the still air. Mae was watching my every move, concentrating more on my well-being than the viewing pleasure ahead. This was either a positive, since she was witnessing an epic sacrifice, or a negative because she was counting the minutes until she never had to deal with this crap again.

The Huey could only seat five, and Mae and I belted into the lone passenger row behind the pilot and co-pilot's seats. Mae sat by the right window and I intentionally sat with my butt cheeks precisely straddling the exact midpoint. Tom had us put on large wired headsets to communicate with each other and block out the imminent deafening rotor, engine, and wind noise. I had an unwanted, unobstructed view of the two-dozen gauges and switches on the instrument panel; complexities I would prefer to be ignorant of. My anxious expression reflected back at me from all of the windows. Mae grabbed my hand and said a quick prayer for safety, which used to ease my tension a notch.

Tom flipped a few switches and the two massive rotor blades above whirled counter-clockwise, as did the smaller vertically mounted tail rotor. Even the well-insulated headsets could not block out all of the intense mechanical orchestration creating our lift. In less than two minutes we were hovering ten feet off the helipad, and then, without the long-drawn-out pageantry of a plane take-off, we soared into the sky. Although nervous, I remained relatively calm since it was so smooth, and we leveled off at a comforting one hundred feet. It was not ideal plowing through low-visibility fog, but it was sparse enough beneath us to provide clear views of the treetops and scenery. Tom narrated in a soothing voice, explaining what he was doing and where we presently were. I assumed he was oversharing since he likely had extensive experience with nervous passengers—except, what pilot snuck shots of Jack to their cargo?

Though my preference was to know as little as possible about what kept us from crashing, Mae was curious and Tom was happy to explain. When I was a kid I got a similar lesson from an older cousin who was stationed at Camp Pendleton during Vietnam. Tom's right hand maneuvered a stick between his legs controlling the tilt of the main rotor for direction; his left hand worked a lever controlling the pitch of the main blades for lift; and both feet worked pedals controlling the pitch of the tail blades for left and right steering.

A few minutes into our approximately forty-minute round-trip, I noticed the distance from the ground increasing. When I asked Tom if this was a mistake he assured me there were minimum altitude requirements when flying over the canyon itself. Flying inside the canyon had been banned because of noise pollution. Soon, because of the fog, we could not see in front, or below us, and both my hands gripped the seat tightly in anticipation of the additional vertical nothingness beneath. It killed me how Mae's facial expression was no different than it would be on It's a Small World. Tom was humming Richard Wagner's "The Ride of the Valkyries."

The fog in front brightened, and then thinned, and then *boom*, the sun and blue sky, which had evaded us all weekend, blinded us. Like a small rodent looking all around to make sure he was not instant prey, I tried to get my bearings. Behind us was a wall of fog masking the south rim, and in every other direction were the canyon's glorious, multi-color, layered valleys, mesas, ridges, and buttes, with a frosting of snow on the higher stripes. The breath-taking view counterbalanced my new perspective of thousands of feet of nothing under my two.

I knew exactly where we were before Tom briefed us. The butte, Battleship Rock, was on our left, and we did not appear to be much higher than the ridgeline. Directly beneath was the widening mesa of the Tonto Platform. We must have entered the canyon over the Bright Angel Fault because we were following the faint line of the Bright Angel trail. When we passed over Indian Garden, it seemed as much of a riparian green mirage from the sky as it did from the trail, only from this vantage people looked more like ants. Mae's dimples dented as she took it all in. Instead of veering right with the Bright Angel trail, Tom took us over Plateau Point at the end of the Tonto Platform, revealing the innermost gorge and the snaking blue-green Colorado. Over the river he smoothly turned us upstream towards the sand-colored pointed spire, the Zoroaster Temple butte, in the far distance.

When we turned left over the Silver Suspension Bridge, Mae's left hand found and tightened around my right, severing the remaining threads of my anxiety. This was a *great* idea. We followed the Bright Angel Creek and saw the campgrounds, mule corral, cabins, canteen, picnic tables, and mature cottonwoods of Phantom Ranch. With each triggered memory she squeezed my hand tighter, affirming her recollection of our inspiring beginning and the promise it offered. Further up Bright Angel Creek we turned left over the narrower Phantom Canyon and creek. The large pool on top of the waterfall earned another squeeze and Mae commented,

Lolly, lolly, lolly, get your adverbs here, and I replied, *Thank you, sir. May I have another?* This earned a drowsy *dyn-o-mite* from Tom, who had gone quiet when it became obvious we were in familiar territory.

We got a nice view of the North Rim Village before Tom u-turned and steered us back south again. After reconnecting with the Colorado he turned right and paralleled the river bends, and soon we were unmistakably above the Horn Creek Rapid and the upstream beach Mae fell in from. This prompted her hand to vice grip mine, and she was smiling and gently crying at the same time. As we turned left back over the Tonto Platform, *it* returned in its entire splendor—the long-gone glow my heart had ached for. The illuminated interior of the helicopter made me feel like I was inside a kid's nightlight. Even though I was trapped in an old Vietnam-era Huey, painted in a fried breakfast theme, thousands of feet in the air, with a potentially drunk pilot, I was *exactly* where I wanted to be.

As we approached Indian Garden, I noticed how I was able to ascertain so much more detail than I could on our earlier fly-over. This time I could easily determine hair and clothing color of campers and hikers. Mae's glow dimmed a bit and she was leaning forward and looking at Tom, curious about something. I looked around the left side of his seat and saw his left hand resting on the lever that controlled our lift. Through the windshield, in the not too far distance, I could see the wall of fog we would need to disappear into again. While Mae leaned forward, I looked out her window and noticed our perspective of Battleship Rock was from below, not above like last time.

"Tom," Mae said. He did not answer. She said it three times more, escalating in volume until he stirred and apologized for *resting* his eyes.

"Tom," I said, "should Battleship Rock be above us?"

After looking over at Battleship Rock, and then at his altimeter, our professional pilot exclaimed, *what the fuck*, the same moment the fog bank swallowed us. No soothing explanation was given this time as he gradually pulled back on the stick and pushed up on the lever and we immediately climbed blindly through the murkiness. Mae's inner light was doused as she matched my fright level. Seconds later, our view cleared enough to reveal a steep face of Redwall limestone with the Jacob's Ladder switchbacks Zorro'ing down it—less than a hundred yards out.

"Hold on!" Tom shouted as he jerked the stick back more and thrust the lever up, maximizing our lift as our angle steepened from a freeway ramp to an A-frame roof.

Shoved deep into our seats by gravity, hands still locked, as the Huey shook in aggravation, Mae and I responded to Richard Dawson's request to name the most common expletives used in a helicopter crash. The limestone was rapidly approaching. The shaking worsened, and Mae grabbed my head to look at hers.

When our shaky eyes met, she purposefully yelled her last ever words to me, "No matter what, we were meant to fall in love and try to be together. It's an undeniable truth in my heart."

I yelled back, "Meeting you was the best thing I've ever done."

She showed me her dimples one last time. "I love you."

I smiled, content that we were leaving this world together, thus avoiding ever missing each other. "I love you, too."

Our ride, slowing to a speed not able to support flight, felt and sounded like a shaking jigsaw puzzle box. The canyon was finally going to claim its victims after many failed attempts. We braced for the crash.

28. '79

It was the fastest, and only, tie-down roping I had ever seen done with a Borg headband, and Chad's right forearm was now locked to Anne's left. The defeated look on her face gave way to one of astonishment. If she plunged, he plunged. He powerfully drove the heels of his boots down into the impermeable earth, making just enough of a ledge for leverage. Then he used every bit of strength his powerful legs had, and did not have, to do his best David Banner–into–the Hulk conversion. I was reinvigorated and used a power surge to pull with an effort I felt could tear her arm at the socket. Mae had switched to my side, laid flat on her stomach with her head and arms precariously over the edge, and was trying to pull Anne up from the armpit. Grace under fire Kurt Russell was still scrambling around in the background.

Anne's left shoulder resurfaced, followed by her right. Her gray tank did little to shield her flesh from the carving nature of the sharp rock; her neck and upper chest looked like they had been swiped by a mountain lion. With Anne more secure, Chad leaned forward and slipped his left arm around her upper arm and gave a mighty heave. Her breasts returned, deeply gouged. Now all three of us pulled her up from the armpits and were able to get her upper torso on the shelf. She threw her left knee up and Chad grabbed it and pulled while Mae and I continued on her upper body. Both legs came up and she lunged safely away from the ledge and collapsed from exhaustion. Chad, Mae, and I followed suit.

Kurt Russell stood over us. His Waffelos shaded my face. "Are you guys okay?"

We all looked at him in utter bewilderment.

Anne answered in between deep breaths, "Fuck you, Kurt Russell, and your fucking mini-waffles." Her remark triggered irrepressible laughter in all, except Kurt, and stunted our ability to recapture our lung capacity.

As we recovered and readied for the end of our trek, Anne thanked us bigheartedly and showed off the deep scratches and bruises all over her body, including the ones our fingernails left, and the large round purple bruise Chad's head imprinted in her left bun yesterday. Kurt Russell, whom *we* ignored, left for Indian Garden with his cereal. Chad strangely did not have his pack, though, even stranger, did have his stereo. He offered to carry Anne's pack. His greatly stretched headband was around his neck like a collar. Mae and I, and especially Anne, were anxiously waiting for him to address the elephant in the canyon before we embarked.

"I owe all of you a deep apology," he began. "Especially Anne. There's absolutely no excuse for how I ditched you."

"You're right," Anne said with a poker face.

"I admit I'm a bastard for cheating on my fiancée weeks before our wedding," he said. "I'm processing what I'm going to do with this information. Anne, I want you to know I meant every word I said to you down there. Every compliment and expression of my feelings, and even the cheesy stuff during sex."

"Then why did you leave?" Anne asked.

"Because it scared the shit out of me. I had no doubts about my upcoming marriage until I met you. Now I'm overwhelmed by them."

"And?" Anne asked expectantly.

"And...I'm going through with it. You and I are fantastic together, but so are Suzy and I. It all comes down to timing. If we met when we were both single, like Kevin and Mae, things would be different."

I delayed my reaction a second to avoid being too obvious, then glanced over at Mae. Her stare and dimples were waiting for me.

"And once you invest a ton of time into creating a strong, long-lasting relationship," Chad continued, "I think those are the relationships we should commit to, instead of seeking alternatives. Ultimately, I asked Suzy to spend the rest of her life with me, and she happily and eagerly accepted that proposal. And...that's not an agreement I'm willing to break. Sorry."

Anne had tears on her face, but you could tell she respected his decision. She wrapped her arms around him *and* the pack, easily clasping her hands together, and kissed him on the forehead.

"Maybe Paul Bunyan's single?" Chad said.

"Kiss my grits," she said, smiling, and pushed him away.

"Where's your pack?" Mae asked.

"I left it at the rim. My hiking partner, guilt, decided we needed to come back and find you. I couldn't leave you hanging." Chad smiled.

"You're so square," Anne said.

"Why did you bring your stereo?" I asked.

"For this," he said, and struggled to pull a cassette tape out of his tight cord shorts. He handed it to Anne to read the label.

"No way. Far out," she said.

"What does it say?" Mae asked.

"*Only Play in Emergency—Chad's Way Cool Disco.*"

Anne popped in the tape. Chad stopped her before she pressed play.

"What?" she asked.

"First you have to teach us your funky arm dances so we can flap along."

"There's nothing to teach," she said. "Do whatever comes naturally."

For the final three steep miles of our escape from the canyon, Chad and Anne clapped, drummed, flapped, hand jived, pointed, rolled, waved, air guitar'd, air piano'd, bowled, climbed a ladder, cowbell'd, delivered mail, knocked, painted, pushed the lawnmower, rolled dough, shined shoes, shopped in a grocery store, put the groceries away, shotput, shot skeet, sprinkler headed, swam different strokes, did *the hustle* and some *kung fu fighting*, declared they were *born to be alive, makin' it, hot stuff,* and *dancing queen*s, told each other *you should be dancing, everyone's a winner, I will survive, don't leave me this way, take a chance on me,* and *knock on wood,* strolled through *MacArthur Park* and a *disco inferno,* and celebrated their surviving a *tragedy* with their *last dance.*

Mae and I were only bit background players while Chad and Anne headlined the Bright Angel trail disco concert. We had gotten the performing out of our systems yesterday and were happy to witness our friends demonstrating how fun life can be if you dropped your inhibitions and experienced pure escapism. Mae rode this infectious wave of positivity, and our quarrels from earlier had been cleanly left millions of years deeper in the canyon. I proposed she pay a visit to San Diego, or I pay a visit to Phoenix, sometime this summer. She concurred, but noticeably did not offer any further suggestive details to help convert the plan to reality. A layer preventing her feelings from fully connecting with mine remained. And the possibility loomed larger that I was overestimating the depth of her feelings.

As we stepped foot on the rim and passed the rail I had almost flipped over, the four of us stopped, turned around, looked down into the canyon and back in time, and quietly reflected on our weekend. It was one I would never forget for many powerful reasons, and I assumed the others felt the same way. I felt that the best of me had arisen down there, and I wanted to be sure to take it with. We all slowly rotated, away from our past, and faced the terrain and buildings of the South Rim Village. *Crap!* I had to start the grown-up part of my life now.

The girls agreed to join us for a late lunch in the El Tovar Lounge before driving back to Phoenix. Except for a few patrons sitting at the bar, the handful of cocktail tables and chairs were empty—great weather was a deterrent for indoor drinking. The four of us sat at a table next to a large picture window facing the canyon. All flavors of tourists were abuzz on the rim. From the overhead speakers, Kenny Rogers kept affirming *she believes in me.*

When the bartender, *Tom* per nametag, a tall, skinny Native American a little older than us, with a ponytail and bad acne, dropped off menus, he was not shy about expressing his infatuation with our stereo, which Chad had brought in with him. Chad ordered a round of Miller Lites, which the girls offered no opposition to. I overheard Tom excitedly telling his counter customers he just received his helicopter pilot's license earlier today and his tour business was officially open.

We ordered six cheeseburgers; two for Chad since he hiked six miles farther than we did, and two for Anne just because. Conversation gradually returned to unadventurous college bar chitchat, slowly deteriorating the feeling of invincibility from when we surfaced on the rim. Chad excused himself and asked if I could step out to the lobby with him.

Once outside the lounge, he spoke to me in a hushed tone, "Your only chance with this girl is if you do something unexpected and out of character—something with an immediate impact."

"I was going to get her number and see if we could schedule a weekend together in Phoenix or S.D.," I said.

"Do something different, bolder," he said.

My head spun. I glanced uneasily at the mounted vicious-tusked javelina eavesdropping on our conversation. My future had become a temperamental bomb ready to detonate any second, and I needed to figure out which random wire to cut, even though I was engrained to always cut the red one.

"Do you have any suggestions?" I asked.

"Use the force."

"Fuck you. I'm serious."

"And when that fails, pray on it," he said, and headed back into the lounge.

I followed his advice.

When I returned to the lounge, with tunnel vision on my goal, I angled towards the bar instead of our table. I congratulated Tom on his helicopter pilot's license and asked whether he was ready for his first customers, today, right now.

29. '01

Tom slammed his left foot down and pulled the stick to the left. We turbulently banked at a snail's pace, and out my window I got a slow motion, shingle-counting, up-close view of the pitched roof of the three-mile resthouse. Mae unlocked our hands to further brace herself—a logical move, but one I insecurely took personally—as the Huey attempted the u-turn. With help from its enemy, now turned friend, gravity, our craft picked up speed as it slid down the opposite roof of the A-frame, then got on a freeway ramp, and eventually returned to a level eastern flight path, sightlessly through the fog. An aircraft ski jump into the abyss did little to calm me down, and I was still convinced we were going to smash into something, but Tom seemed comfortable again after triple-checking his altimeter and headings, and we were rewarded by bursting out of the haze into wide-open sky safely above the Tonto Platform.

As Indian Garden came into view again, Tom took us to a higher altitude while guiltily apologizing. I had gripped the seat so tightly my fingernails partially ripped out of their beds. I could not relax until I was safely on the ground, but I loosened my right hand and sought Mae's. She was breathing deeply, trying to calm herself, and apparently didn't notice the hand offering. I put it on her right leg, which sparked a half-smile, brief lash flutter, and shallow dimples, but did not trigger either of her hands to free up. I returned my hand to its previous indentation in the seat. Though this was an extreme, unchartered set of circumstances, it somehow felt like Mae had suddenly distanced herself. I was probably in shock and overthinking everything.

After leveling off, well above the peak of Battleship Rock, Tom slowly u-turned us again back towards the south rim. I eagerly awaited Mae to acknowledge me in any manner. I needed something—anything—a single remnant of the glowing love she recalled and reignited shortly before our near catastrophe. As I readied my hand for another attempt, we flew into the south rim's gray blanket. I was sick of playing peek-a-boo canyon. This time, though the Huey's interior temperature did not drop, my clouded vision was accompanied by an onset of inner chills. By the time Tom, who was now nervously overcompensating with excess narrative, announced we were past the rim, I was shaking uncontrollably. It was as if one of my layers ceased to exist beyond the boundaries of the canyon. Mae noticed and gave me a sympathetic quick pat on the leg, then returned her gaze to the front and hand to its previous resting spot. As we descended through the fog and then skirted over the treetops, I continued to tremble. By the time we touched down on the helipad, my teeth were chattering violently and I could barely control my hands enough to remove my headset. As Tom powered down, Mae returned her attention to me and kept saying I would be all right. Inexplicably, I felt worse now than when I thought we were going to crash. It was almost as if we *did* crash but I had yet to fully comprehend it. I took a handful of deep breaths and calmed enough to unbuckle and climb out.

"I imagine you'd like your money back," Tom said dolefully.

My present feelings for Tom were mixed since the only reason he was able to miraculously save us was because he almost killed us.

"I'd offer you a voucher for a future flight," he continued, "but I'm fairly certain they're going to make me retire today." His tone affirmed he was at peace with it. "But drinks are on me the rest of your stay. My shift at the El Tovar Lounge starts in a half hour."

Mae drove on the way back since I was physically a bit off. Unlike after the mule deer incident, we did not share a deep cry or hearty laugh to celebrate being alive. We drove in complete silence. She pulled into the visitor center lot and parked in the same spot as two days ago when we arrived, by the trailhead to Mather Point. The trail to the rocky outcrop and view area was bustling with tourists ready for the fog to burn off at any moment.

"You want to go sightseeing?" I said to her disbelievingly.

She was looking away from me, out her window. "Kevin, I need to spend a little time alone. Do you mind walking around a bit while I decompress at the hotel?"

Her request was a little odd, but I wanted to be accommodating. "Why don't I go back with you and hang in the lobby or lounge while you regroup?" I asked.

She was still looking away from me and didn't answer.

"Mae, what's wrong? Can you please look at me?"

She turned with a full smile, but tears rolled down her cheeks and temporarily pooled in her dimples. "Nothing's wrong, Kevin. A girl just needs time alone once in a while. I'll pick you up in an hour. I'll be all right. And you'll be all right, okay?"

"Okay," I said.

She leaned in for a kiss, and when our lips met she closed her eyes and held the back of my head for an extended period of time. When she pulled away, she took in a large breath and stared forward. I got out of the car and waved, as she pulled away without turning her head.

The northern, eastern, and western protective railings border-ing Mather Point's seventy-five-foot jetty of Kaibab limestone were lined with tourists, as was most of the rim trail of the South Rim Village. Everybody waited in anticipation, as if the sunrise, sunset, or another timely event, like fireworks or a CCR reunion, were about to take place. The growing light behind the gray curtain ver-ified the performance would begin any moment. Thick snow still covered the area between the rim trail and the canyon's precipice, creating a dangerous vagueness to where the true canyon's edge began. The chipmunks were out in full force, working the crowd with extra cuteness to replenish their diminished resources from two days of no tips. I waited on the rim trail just west of Mather. I felt no need to join the masses on the crowded outcrop with sheer drops and risk a tour group jamming me against the edge while their guide rambled on about the first director of the National Park Service.

I opened my Velcro wallet, a birthday present from my kids I felt was too casual for someone my age, and took out an extremely weathered, folded piece of paper. I unfolded it. The first three words, *travel, explore,* and *experience,* were crossed out. Then, writ-ten with three underlines beneath it for emphasis, was *Happy Old Age.* I often retrieved this little note for inspiration. I thought back to when Mae and I decided to write down the object of the game for our lives in the Phantom Ranch canteen on the first day we met, and then lost our answers. It was not until I returned to San Diego and washed my red dirt–stained clothes that I found her answer jammed deep in the pocket of my cord shorts. I had never told Mae I found it. It was silly, but I had envisioned giving it to her many years down the road, perhaps on our fiftieth wedding anniversary, when we were in the heart of what those three simple words represented. Today, I planned to use the note as part of the final plea to my wife to not leave me. It was the original plea I had planned before Chad convinced me to *do something different*;

something that nearly killed us, but left me no more the wiser to whether Mae would wake up next to me every morning for the rest of our lives.

As soon as Mae returned from the hotel, I planned to guide her by hand to the end of Mather Point and lead her in a slow dance, while quietly serenading her with the words to a sentimental song. If the production values were absolutely perfect, at the precise moment of the canyon's awe-inspiring unveiling, I would slip the weathered note into her hand. When her heavy lashes rose, eyes widened, and dimples deepened from the recognition, I would promise to rededicate the rest of my life—of *our* life—to helping *us* reach the square of *Happy Old Age* together.

I glanced around at the multitudes of onlookers. No one else looked as lost as I felt. They were all here for a reason, with a purpose, and not because their spouse kicked them out of the car at the nearby trailhead. They were waiting for much more than a large hole to reveal itself. Ponch's observation was accurate: *I think seeing it gives people faith that if something so beautiful can be created out of rock, then think of what can be done with you.* You could see it not only in their wide-open eyes, but also their wide-open souls, which stood ready to take in whatever the canyon offered; a longing for the physical big void to replace any emotional voids in their own lives. And in these precious moments leading up to their preconceived moment, their minds were in overdrive contemplating what they wanted out of life.

There was an orange safety cone nearby because of a large splintered pine branch felled during the weekend storm. I considered picking it up and using it as a megaphone to lecture the crowds: *The Grand Canyon is an example of what not to do in life. Strengthen the layers of your foundation, and prevent them from eroding away.*

Close to an hour after I arrived, with the canyon implausibly still too stubborn to drop its final thin veil, I heard footsteps approach from behind. My face brightened in anticipation. Then I heard the footsteps detour off the path into softer dirt, branches rustling, water streaming to the ground, and light-saber sound effects. All hope escaped from my mind, all feeling from my heart, and I closed my eyes.

"Hey, Chad," I said without turning.

"Hey, buddy," he said compassionately.

"When did Mae ask you to drive out?" I asked.

"It was touch and go all weekend, but this morning. I was sworn to secrecy. I'm so sorry."

"I understand," I said. I still could not turn to face him, for it would confirm the reality of what was happening.

"We were praying as we drove that you would make a miraculous comeback before we got here," he said. "Sounds like you came close, especially if you'd prefer ending both your lives instead of spending them apart."

"Where is she now?" I asked.

"She and Anne left about fifteen minutes ago. She's going to stay with us in Phoenix for a little while. She didn't want you to be alone, so I can drive back to Diego with you and hang for a few days if you'd like."

"Who's watching your twins?"

"Her mom. I know I'm here under shitty circumstances, but thank you for the hall pass. I brought mushrooms just in case."

This warranted a turn away from the canyon. "Are you serious?"

"Sorry. Not funny," he said.

Chad had aged well, wore his hair in the style of his youth, and was nostalgically wearing his Fila Borg headband and carrying his old stereo. He was smiling, knowing how silly he looked with his accessories.

"Anne had to cut six inches out of the headband and re-sew it after I saved her ass with it," he said. "And as I suspected twenty-two years ago, that bartender/pilot, Tom, stole my stereo. I just found it on the bar in the El Tovar Lounge. He even admitted to it. I should have been pissed at the guy, but I felt sorry for him."

A spattering of clapping began. It quickly morphed into a thunderous applause accompanied by cheering. The star of the show had made its triumphant return. I could not believe I would always remember applause and cheering at the moment I knew my wife left me. Tears arrived in droves. Without Mae's light, how would I avoid spending the rest of my life in darkness? There was no need for me to turn to see the Grand Canyon, now a heartrending reminder that I had eroded a deep, permanent hole and void in my life. *Given enough time, nothing is more changeable than rock.*

30. '79

Tom thought I was kidding until I pulled out a wad of cash I had saved for the rest of our trip and gas. I unfortunately underestimated the expense of flying, especially with the current oil crisis. He told me the other two tour companies were charging $150 per head for forty-five-minute tours. He asked me if I had any plastic, and I hesitantly pulled out my dad's Master Charge Interbank card I was only supposed to use in case of emergencies.

"Three hundred bucks for the four of us," I offered.

"Five fifty and your friend's groovy stereo," he countered.

"Three fifty and no stereo."

"Four fifty and the stereo."

"Four without, and that's my final offer."

"Dyn-o-mite!" he said, quick enough for me to realize I over-paid. "Meet me in a half hour at the airport in the building by the helipad." He grabbed my dad's Master Charge.

I told Chad and the girls I had excess bachelor party funds I felt obligated to blow through and just found the perfect vehicle. They were all thrilled at the prospect of the helicopter tour. Chad's grin displayed he knew very well this was not being done in his honor, but he did not give a hoot. As Chad and I followed in my Cutlass behind the girls' Volkswagen Bug, which followed behind Tom's truck, on the way to the Grand Canyon Airport, he and I cranked up the radio and sang along to "Convoy"—Chad's deep voice was a perfect Rubber Duck. Since it was on the way out of town, the girls planned to leave for Phoenix from there.

Two old Vietnam Hueys, one freshly painted red, the other freshly painted yellow, were parked on the apron next to a helipad occupied with an original military-green Huey with a brown, red, orange, and yellow scene painted on the side. We walked by the adjoining offices of three tour companies. Tom explained that two ex-military pilots were his competition, and he was sure he would be the first to expand and update his fleet and hire more pilots. We opened the door to his single-room office with four new upholstered foldout chairs and a desk area. He had thumbtacked up two concert promotion posters from an L.A. band he saw at a couple of clubs when he was in Riverside getting his license. He swore this group, Van Halen, was going to be huge, and Chad and I agreed since we had caught a few of their shows. He said he would replace the cheap foldout waiting chairs along with the posters and other furnishings as soon as the big bucks rolled in. And he wanted to get a stereo, like Chad's, so he could pump up his customers with his favorite tunes before each flight.

While we followed him out to the helipad, he explained that when he had turned twenty-one he used a tribal inheritance to get licensed and put a down payment on the Huey. So many of his tribesmen held key positions in the Grand Canyon area that he was sure to be flooded with referrals. He would bartend at the El Tovar Lounge to supplement his income until the business ramped up. He asked us what we thought of his recent painting on the side of the Huey, which he had done himself. We all agreed it was a frying pan, though the girls thought it was hash browns and sausage, while Chad and I voted eggs and bacon. We felt awkward when he explained it was supposed to be a canyon vista at sunrise. He said he'd also correct this when the big bucks rolled in.

We maxed out his passenger capacity with Chad in the co-pilot's seat and Anne, Mae, and me in the three-person backseat. A switch in Mae had been flipped ever since I hatched this plan, and her eyes and dimples showed no signs that this was our last hurrah. Tom had us put on large wired headsets to communicate with each other and block out the rotor, engine, and wind noise. The many windows reflected all of our war wounds from the weekend. Tom powered up and the overhead and tail-rotor blades slowly came to life. He excitedly told us we could fly fairly low into the canyon, but due to tourist complaints they were considering a much higher fly zone in the future.

As the Huey's energy and noise increased, and I knew any second we would begin to hover, I flashed back to almost flipping over the railing, nervously cliff jumping, witnessing Chad's disappearance in the flash flood, Mae's and my near-drowning in the river, and Anne's delirious river-jump attempt and accidental slide over the precipice. Going into this weekend, I felt momentum-less, but after these events I felt dangerously out of control. My palms started to sweat, my heart beat in double-time, and I felt a collapsing pressure on my chest. I could tell I was on the verge of a panic attack and knew I needed to eject before the liftoff set it in full motion.

"Tom, hold up," I said. "I'm so sorry. I can't do this."

Everyone responded with light encouragements, assuming I was only a little nervous. They realized the severity when I avoided eye contact, took off my headset, and opened the door.

"Chad, I'll hitch back," I said. "You can take the Cutlass. I'll wait at Mather Point and try to see you in the air."

Everybody's mouth was agape.

"Catch you on the flip-side," Anne said.

"Good luck in Moscow," I said, then turned to Mae.

Mae looked like a four-year-old who just lost her parents in the mall.

"Bye," I said. I tried to be bold, but my current fear shook my voice, "Can you give Chad your number before you leave? Maybe we could see each other again."

Her face didn't register any of it. She was frozen.

I was about to repeat myself when Tom said I needed to exit quickly, and stay low. I had to painfully break eye contact with Mae and rip my heart away. My old *wasn't-meant-to-be* crutch was awaiting as I exited, dispiritedly ducking to avoid the flexing, whirling blade.

"Kevin, wait a minute," Chad shouted.

I turned. He was running after me. I stopped comfortably beyond the radius of the blade and waited for him.

"Don't be down on yourself for skipping this," he said. "I feel a little shaky myself after all of the chaos we've been through. You already blew out the boundaries of your comfort zone this weekend and should feel good about that. Hold your head up high and we'll end the weekend in style tonight."

I looked over his shoulder at Mae.

Chad shook his head. "Don't base your self-worth on a weekend fling not turning into a relationship. That's stupid. The reason you're my best man and will always be my best friend is because spending time with you and your ideals makes me, and most everyone you meet, better. You're a quality guy, Kevin, and if she doesn't recognize that, it's her loss. Wake up from the insecure delusion you're under and accept that you're worthwhile."

"Thanks, buddy. Seriously, thanks," I said, feeling a little better.

Chad remained in place and was silent.

"What?" I asked.

"Damn, Kevin! I'm totally confused on this Anne and Suzy thing."

"I thought you made up your mind."

"So did I, but I'm wavering. What should I do?"

"The same thing you told me to do."

He smiled. "Use the force?"

"And when that fails, pray on it."

"I'll pick you up at Mather Point," he said, then ran back and boarded the helicopter, put on his headset, and gave Tom a thumbs up.

Mae looked out at me and pressed her forehead against the window. My eyes stayed locked on hers as the Huey hovered briefly before angling off.

After hitching a ride to Mather Point, I viewed part of their helicopter tour from afar. Observing how smooth it looked, I deeply regretted my decision. The sightseeing I could have cared less about; it was forfeiting additional time with Mae that made me remorseful. Not to mention, the large Master Charge bill was going to be an unpleasant father/son talk.

I waited for Chad on a bench overlooking the crowded rock jetty. With Mae's chapter ending, my mind had no more excuses to avoid the terrifying reality that I had *no* idea what I wanted to do with my life. As I sat there, I began to feel light-headed, and the canyon began swirling in front of me, likely from the accumulation of physical, emotional, and mental exhaustions. I closed my eyes to make it stop, but then I began to hear and see unfamiliar scenes featuring Mae and me. It was a new chapter, and although Mae looked similar to how she did today, it must have been many years in the future because I looked a lot more like my dad, even donning his haircut I swore I never would. The images were so vivid, detailed, and fluent that I had no reason to question (except to affirm my sanity) their validity. My previous revelations were soft, vague, gentle reminders when compared to this loud, concise, rude awakening. We now had college-aged kids, and in a last-gasp effort to save what had evolved into a failed marriage, we were back at the Grand Canyon trying to rediscover our beginnings. Bad weather and an incomprehensible invisibility of the canyon limited our activities, but our harsh canyon luck continued when Mae nearly crashed the Cutlass, which we strangely still owned, and we came horrifyingly close to going down in a helicopter. There were a lot of familiar faces and, oddly, a special guest star, Willie Aames, whom I sang with.

Although I had no basis to conclude whether this glimpse was grounded in any looming reality, the pain and disappointment I felt from seeing my potential future shortfalls as a husband, as a Christian, and as a man, along with the guilt of how those impacted another's life, could not have felt more real. I was not surprised in the least when, at the end of this new chapter, Mae ultimately left the person I had become. The weight of what I just witnessed was crushing, and my hands instinctually grasped at the edge of the bench to make sure I did not fall into the canyon.

I shook my head, attempting to disrupt and dislodge the lingering heartache, and opened my eyes so my mind could no longer project the hurtful visuals onto the backsides of my eyelids. I was relieved to discover I was wearing my *I'm a Pepper* t-shirt, safely in the summer of 1979, the end of my sheltered youth, the dawn of decisions with life-altering consequences. I used my sense of touch, running my hand through my Jimmy Connors hairstyle, for final tangible confirmation that I was still twenty-two and the rest of my life was unwritten.

Someone approached the bench from the rim trail and called out my name. The dimples, freckles, thick eyelashes, and white embroidered peasant top all unmistakably belonged to Mae, now standing in front of me like a mirage. It took me a few moments before I seized the reality of her presence.

"What are you doing here? I thought you were driving back to Phoenix after the helicopter tour?" I asked.

"I didn't like how we said goodbye," she said.

"Where are Anne and Chad?"

"Waiting in the parking lot."

"Sorry I made an ass of myself back at the helicopter. How was it?" I asked.

"I guess it was fun, but my heart wasn't in it. I recognized, and can relate to, that out of control look in your eyes back there. I'm not going to stand on a podium and say it's square you felt afraid."

"Thank you."

"Kevin, you're a really nice guy and good person."

Nice and *good* were kisses of death.

She continued, "You graduated and we don't live in the same city, or even the same state. And truthfully, I came here this weekend to escape, *not* to be found. We barely know each other. There's no way we could work out."

I detected a strong trace of doubt in her voice.

"Mae, you do realize you're not entitled to dump someone you aren't going out with?" I said, and smiled.

"If you would have seen the look on your face as the helicopter took off," she said. "It was as if you were losing a part of yourself—a part of your future. And...I felt the exact same way. However you want to define it, there's a connection between us."

"Like you said, though, it doesn't matter," I said. "We're logistically challenged. So, whether you'd like to admit it or not, there *is* a rational thinker inside of you."

I overheard Chad in the distance talking with Anne, "I swear I left my stereo in the Cutlass. I bet Tomahawk stole it. Probably still mad we took his land."

"But unlike you, Kevin, I also have a little bit of crazy in me," Mae said. "I want to grow and change, and test the limits of what I can do. I had to push you into Phantom Creek, and I think the only reason you put on a river concert was because you knew your opportunity with me was over if you didn't. I'm concerned someone I have to always push is going to eventually resist. And then I'm going to resent them."

"I was the one who got us on the helicopter, regardless of whether I backed out," I said in my defense.

"I know. I was excited you did that," she said.

"I also insanely jumped into the Colorado to save you."

"And *that's* the main reason why I'm standing in front of you. I feel safe with you. I didn't realize how good that could feel until I felt it. Also, you're grounded and stand up for what you believe in. You're far from a typical twenty-two-year-old."

"Well, it's what we *nice* and *good* guys do. I've got a shelf full of participation trophies. And I thought you were standing in front of me to say why I'm all wrong for you."

"I am. I mean I'm not. Shit, Kevin, I don't know what I'm doing."

"Mae, I only suggested we visit each other this summer," I said.

"Fuck you," she said. "If I'm going to put myself out here like this, fully exposed and vulnerable, then you'd better admit the extent of your feelings right now or I'm leaving."

As I looked as deep into her eyes as I could, the words came easier than I thought, and felt as natural as breathing, "I'm in love with you, Mae."

She held my gaze but did not respond. I had hoped for at least a hint of a glow, but got nothing. Even now, after I confessed, she needed more. She sat down next to me.

"Can you please tell me what's to stop you, or me, or *us*, from fucking things up like our parents did?" she asked. "You said you have visions; what guarantees can you give about our future?" Her face yearned for a meaningful answer.

A potentially validating detail of my vision lingered. "Did you ever remember what you wrote in the canteen for the object of the game, for your life?" I asked.

"No," she said.

"Was it *Happy Old Age*?" Please be wrong.

"Yeah, that was it," she said excitedly. "Did you find the piece of paper?"

"I think I do in the future," I said forlornly.

"And?" she asked, eyes widening in fear, realizing this key opened the door to the larger answer.

This was insane; I just confessed my love and was about to follow it up with *we're doomed*—based on an intangible glimpse? While I struggled over what to say next, a revelation struck—why was I considering this vision a *burden*? Since when was a chance to correct mistakes not yet made a detriment? I'm sure both Mae's and my parents would have been overjoyed to receive such invaluable information early in their relationships. It was an answer to the serenity prayer, *God, grant me the serenity to accept the things I cannot change, the courage to change the things I can, and the wisdom to know the difference.* God gave me the ability to prophesy because He had faith in using me as a vessel to share His wisdom. It was also the perfect opportunity to do what Chad suggested, *something different, bolder,* but on a much bigger platform—my life—and to stay committed to a growth mindset and avoid the traps of a fixed one. And Thomas Jefferson, arguably wiser than Chad, said *nothing can stop the man with the right mental attitude from achieving his goal.* My expression remained unchanged during contemplation, but Mae's eyes broke and welled over from the further delay. I smiled widely before attempting to deliver a dangerous, negative message in an affirming, positive way.

"I simply didn't live up to the person I promised I would be, and…we didn't make it," I said. I realized my pleased expression made it appear I was gloating over the failure.

Mae's expression drowned in a river of confusion.

I continued, "I've received an extraordinary gift, though. I've seen the errors of my ways and have a chance to fix them."

Mae was still drowning, but intensely focused on my words.

"You asked me what I can guarantee about our future," I said. "I can guarantee everything's *not* going to be perfect and life *will* be challenging. But I can also guarantee I will dedicate myself to building us a solid foundation of love, respect, passion, and faith. Mae, you deserve way more than just *Happy Old Age.*"

Mae stopped crying, but her face was heavy with doubt.

"I don't understand," she said. "You claim you already failed at all of this once. What's to keep that from happening again?" Her look was indecipherable.

"Because I know if I remain focused on prioritizing my relationships with both you *and* God, we won't just survive, but will achieve something inspirational." This would be my *grand*. A sign with this message, at the canyon's edge, would have a monumental impact on many.

I added, "Something our kids will one day aspire to have themselves, not try to avoid."

"Kids?" she asked. "Maybe we should scale this discussion back a bit."

"Sorry. Hypothetical kids."

Still sporting a guarded, directionless expression, she asked, "But, Kevin, you can't guarantee we make it, can you?"

The simple truth was that we had known each other for only three days and, though my heart was ready to answer *yes*, my mind realized there were two lives at stake here, not just mine, and I was not omnipotent. My upbeat tone softened. "No, I can't."

She looked down, in thought. Her heart teeter-tottered with her mind over the railing, and I despondently knew that gravity was based in logic. She raised her eyes, and her mouth attempted to form words, but kept vacillating on which ones. When they came out, it was with purpose, knowing these could be her last ever to me, "Would the future me take this same chance with you again?"

It was a powerful question, and though the assumptive answer was rationally *no*, I felt there had been a definitive response to it, an *undeniable truth*, somewhere in my vision. My face blanked while my mind searched frantically. The moment dragged on, and the future, one direction or another, was on hold. I could tell from her plagued expression, on the verge of tears, that Mae was ready to return to the open arms of despair.

DAY 1

31. '01

Exit north out of San Diego, scale the mountains between Temecula and Palm Springs, speed across desolate desert roads, hang a right at Lake Havasu, cross through the freight-train valleys of northern Arizona, and take a left in Williams. Conversation was light, but sprinkled with observations, discussions, and minor disagreements. A seventies and eighties rock radio station filled any voids. I gazed through my translucent reflection in the windshield, still trying to get used to the beard I grew recently in an attempt to rebel against the businessman I was. I glanced over at Mae in the passenger seat; she looked youthful and relaxed, but a little tired from the long drive.

"Sorry that we didn't fly," I said.

"Don't be," she said. "I love our road trips. It's a nice change." As missions pastor at our church, Mae flew a lot. My job as a real estate agent thankfully kept me grounded.

The temperature display on our dash had been ticking down a degree every ten miles for the last couple of hours. As we passed Bedrock City, a replica of Fred Flintstone's hometown, it dropped into the forties, and converging clouds squeezed out the lone remaining way to blue.

"Fiver, you definitely predicted the weather correctly," Mae said. "Although weather.com deserves an assist." We had packed, at my insistence and to her surprise, heavy jackets, snow gear, and even tire chains, just in case.

A siren elevated from an approaching ambulance, and as it shot by, I led us in a prayer for those in need and those on their way to assist them. I threw in an extra prayer for a safe and fruitful weekend. My palms sweat into the steering wheel as we passed the airport before cruising through Tusayan. As we ascended out of Tusayan, a dense fog settled on the road and surrounding pines.

"Unbelievable, Fiver, again, just like you said," Mae said. "But there's no way it can hide something that big."

"We'll see," I said.

We proceeded with caution and my inner excitement and fear built, and senses heightened, as we neared *it*. The visitor center parking lot was sparsely populated—not a surprise on the cold, off-season December day that I insisted we visit on, for closure.

I missed my old Cutlass's swivel seats as we delicately hauled our cramped legs out of our Audi A4. This was our first time back since we met, and past insecurities were welcoming me with open arms. We slipped on jackets and headed in the opposite direction of the visitor center. The walkway was covered with a fine layer of moisture that would slicken if the temperature dropped any further. Even before we ventured on to the Mather Point rock jetty, the initial disappointment and amazement set in.

"No way," Mae stated. "No fucking way, pardon my adjective. You predicted this would happen twenty-two years ago?"

"I did," I said, trying to act cool, even though I was amazed myself. Two hundred seventy-seven miles long, eighteen miles wide, nearly a mile deep, and the Grand Canyon was nowhere to be seen.

Mae walked to the very end of the outcrop, leaned over the railing, and shouted, "I'm mad as hell and not going to take this anymore!"

I had my first heart attack as she feigned jumping, and my second as I processed her comment. It took me a few seconds to remember our game of quote-and-jump, and to realize that she quoted the signature line from the movie *Network*.

"Can you please stay away from the edge," I said.

"Sorry," she said, and stepped towards the interior of the rock plank. "Fiver, you also predicted this was where and when we'd end our marriage. Or, more specifically, where I'd leave you."

"*That* was the one I was going to try to change," I said. "The weather was out of my control."

"And did you? Change *us*?" Mae asked with a poker face.

I reflected back on all of the accomplishments, failures, joy, and disappointment from the last twenty-two years. Every instance along the way when I thought I had all of the answers, I made myself, and our relationship, vulnerable. But when I would release control and seek help from God and Mae, I felt our foundation was strengthened with new, unerodable layers of depth.

I smiled and said, "I think so."

Her indifferent expression remained.

"What do you think?" I asked anxiously, seeking validation.

She didn't answer right away. I worried if she was uncomfortable with her instinctual reaction.

"What do I think?" she eventually echoed. "Kevin, when we met, you not only saved me from physically drowning, but from emotionally drowning. Your values and dedication have helped shape me, and our relationship, into something I'm extremely proud of. And do you remember when you told me life could be built up with enough meaningful stuff to allow you to reflect on negative stuff from a positive place?"

"I remember," I said. "At the river."

"Well, I'm there, and then some, and I've got you to thank for it."

"You're welcome," I said casually.

"No, Kevin," she said with conviction. "I'm thanking you for my life." Her delivery woke me to the gravity of her words.

"You're welcome," I said in a more reverent tone. The weight of an invisible backpack was instantly lifted. "It's funny, though. I feel like I should be thanking *you* for my life. I knew a life with you would be opportunistic, and it has kept me motivated to constantly work on myself, and us. And, believe it or not, I feel like through that terrifying vision I saw all those years ago, I received an all-too-real sampling of the pain and disappointment I would feel if I ever fell short as a husband, as a Christian, and as a man, along with the guilt of how that would impact your life. Thank you for taking a chance on me."

"You're welcome," she said, and dimpled. "Well…since there's nothing to see out here, I think we should go figure out something to do in the room before Chad and Anne arrive." She sported a mischievous look.

"Do you think she'll bring her costume?" I asked. After the U.S. boycotted the 1980 Moscow Olympics, Anne ended up becoming a professional wrestler nicknamed *The Ann-ihilator.*

"You'd like that, wouldn't you?" she asked. "No, of course she won't bring her costume."

"I'll call Chad and ask him to pack it. If so, will you wear it?" I asked. Chad was Anne's manager, and husband. He even had a bit part in some of her matches, as *The Brawling Borg*, accessorized with a headband he bound her opponents with.

"Pretty sure we're a different spandex size. Come on, Kevin, let's head back to the room. Let's take advantage of our time away from the herd." My mom was watching our four kids back in San Diego.

"You know, we wouldn't have this problem if we had started earlier and stopped at a couple," I said. "They'd be in college and out of the house by now."

"I'm sorry," she said sarcastically. "But did you *not* enjoy our years of marriage and travel before the kids?"

I grinned. She knew I did. Working on the rhythm of our relationship, before working on relationships with kids, was one of our wisest choices. Also, seeing the world was a necessity for Mae's soul, and we had a lot of great memories, even with a few white-knuckle flights.

Residual doubt from a different concern still lingered, and I wasn't ready to leave. I took her left hand in mine.

"Mae, what about the next twenty-two years of our life? I worry that I could still lose focus. Do you ever worry about our future?"

"Kevin, I think it's natural to think about those things. Just so you know, males aren't the only ones with an apathy gene. I think about that once in a while, too. But do I truly worry about us not making it to *Happy Old Age* in the game of life? Absolutely not."

"Why not?" I asked.

She dimpled deeply, began to glow, and displayed a gratified look, the default through her forties. "Because I have faith in *us*."

I could not express in words how wonderful that made me feel. I pulled her in close to me and then angled my eyes into hers.

Her light brightened in recognition. "Are *you* about to *intentionally* do something uncomfortable?" she asked, surprised.

"I thought it would make this moment more memorable. Any requests?"

"I kind of liked the one you picked last time."

I began to sing, *I would...*

DAY 3

32. '79

When I finally found the critical evidence I needed—a piece of her future heart—I prayed the heart standing in front of me possessed the same contents as that one. I took a deep breath and carefully delivered my findings, "In a climatic moment, you said, *no matter what, we were meant to meet, fall in love, and try to be together.*"

Her eyes widened like saucers.

"What?" I asked.

"That's exactly what I felt just now." She was in shock.

"Mae?"

"Yes?" she whispered back.

"I have faith in *us.*"

"And is faith enough?"

"If it remains strong, it can't fail," I said. "And if that doesn't work, we can try using the force."

Mae laughed through tears of hope as she eluded despair's grip. "Kevin, I'm in love with you, too."

Flush with adrenaline, emotion, and another record level of self-realization, I leaned towards her. She surprisingly did not welcome, or lean forward for, an embrace. A devious smile crept onto her face.

She said, "Since you bailed on the helicopter, you need to do something else a little bit crazy; something that will make this moment more memorable."

"Wasn't this whole weekend memorable enough?" I asked.

"Sorry, you're going to have to top it," she said, smiling large.

I recalled from my vision the final plea I had planned to use twenty-two years from now. The more strategic move would be to implement it now, and then spend the next twenty-two years avoiding the need for a final plea at all. I grabbed one of Mae's hands and led her quietly onto Mather Point. Going out seventy-five feet into the canyon, with a sheer drop-off on both sides, felt like walking the plank, and with Mae's missing incisor she looked a little bit like a pirate, in a sexy way. At the end railing I pulled her close to me, into a classic ballroom dancing pose. Our eyes angled into each other's. Her luminosity returned.

"What song would you like?" I asked, self-conscious of the tourists now watching us. Her glow had transformed her into a lighthouse for lost souls.

"Whatever comes naturally," she said.

I led us in a slow dance, and with the help of Foreigner, not the foreigners watching us, I quietly serenaded her, *I would climb any mountain | sail across a stormy sea.*

She laughed in recognition.

I continued, *if that's what it takes me baby | to show you how much you mean to me.* I raised my voice with confidence, *and I guess it's just the woman in you | that brings out the man in me | I know I can't help myself | you're all in the world to me.* I ignored the crescendo and whispered the chorus, *it feels like the first time | feels like the very first time.*

With each line, Mae's inner light shone brighter, validating the life-altering decision she had made, and making me feel unbelievably alive. I pulled her in closer. Even though in that moment I knew, without a doubt, I wanted Mae in my life, my first adult comprehension of the real possibilities of future misdirection, apathy, and change clouded my desires. A lifetime promise was the most powerful, yet most dangerous and susceptible, promise one could make. Since Mae had surrendered her heart and taken a leap of faith, I had to make sure she would not always regret overlooking alternate paths.

"We could still fail," I said with full sincerity.

She leaned back from our embrace and locked her eyes on mine. "Only if we don't try," she said.

We sealed our pact with a long, canyon's edge kiss, and proceeded, together, along the unpredictable, vulnerable, awe-inspiring trail through life.

ACKNOWLEDGEMENTS

Thank you to my test readers who provided valuable feedback: Nicole Brewer, Daniel Burk, Jill Esau, Gregg Foster, Chip Fuller, Kathy Hallock, Alix Kammeyer, Jim Nollsch, Nancy Weinstein, and the Holstens (Andrea, Mom, and Dad). Thank you to Lisa Adlam for another amazing editing job. Thank you to CreateSpace for the interior design of the paperback. Thank you to 52 Novels for another smooth Word to eBook conversion. Thank you to Glenn Jones for his quick and incredible cover work. Thank you to Major Jesse McKeeman for teaching me helicopter basics. Thank you to Wally Marx and Cary Evans for joining me on a random 40th birthday expedition to the Grand Canyon, which, along with a large 70s music file Wally shared, inspired my setting. Thank you to Wikipedia for a whole bunch of 70s and Grand Canyon information that I pray was accurate. Thank you to my parents for always supporting me. Thank you to my kids, who inspire me to want to be better. Thank you to my wife, Andrea, for enduring my late nights of writing, and loving me. And thank you to God for all of the above.

ABOUT THE AUTHOR

Tim Holsten lives with his wife and four children in North County San Diego. His first novel, *The Accidental Bachelor*, was published in 2013. His second effort, *Finding Grand*, resulted from observations of, and experiences in, marriage and faith, a comical 40th birthday trip to the Grand Canyon, and listening to a ton of 70s music really loud.